THE BALLAD OF A BROKEN NOSE

THE BALLAD OF A BROKEN NOSE

Arne Svingen

Translated by Kari Dickson

Margaret K. McElderry Books

New York   London   Toronto   Sydney   New Delhi

MARGARET K. McELDERRY BOOKS
An imprint of Simon & Schuster Children's Publishing Division
1230 Avenue of the Americas, New York, New York 10020
This book is a work of fiction. Any references to historical events, real people, or real places are used fictitiously. Other names, characters, places, and events are products of the author's imagination, and any resemblance to actual events or places or persons, living or dead, is entirely coincidental.
Sangen om en Brukkt Nese copyright © 2012 by Gyldendal Norsk Forlag AS
English translation copyright © 2016 by Simon & Schuster, Inc.
Originally published in Norway in 2012 by Gyldendal Norsk Forlag as *Sangen om en Brukkt Nese*
Published by arrangement with Gyldendal Norsk Forlag
Cover illustration copyright © 2016 by Jensine Eckwall
All rights reserved, including the right of reproduction in whole or in part in any form.
MARGARET K. McELDERRY BOOKS is a trademark of Simon & Schuster, Inc.
For information about special discounts for bulk purchases, please contact Simon & Schuster Special Sales at 1-866-506-1949 or business@simonandschuster.com.
The Simon & Schuster Speakers Bureau can bring authors to your live event. For more information or to book an event, contact the Simon & Schuster Speakers Bureau at 1-866-248-3049 or visit our website at www.simonspeakers.com.
Also available in a Margaret K. McElderry Books hardcover edition
Book design by Sonia Chaghatzbanian
The text for this book was set in Adobe Caslon Pro.
Manufactured in the United States of America
0517 OFF
First Margaret K. McElderry Books paperback edition June 2017
10 9 8 7 6 5 4 3 2 1
CIP data is available from the Library of Congress.
ISBN 978-1-4814-1542-2 (hc)
ISBN 978-1-4814-1543-9 (pbk)
ISBN 978-1-4814-1544-6 (eBook)

THE BALLAD OF A BROKEN NOSE

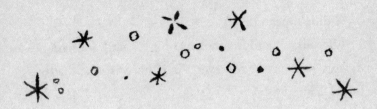

My first chapter

It doesn't matter. These things happen.

I'm lying on the floor. A few seconds ago, I was standing on my feet. The world was on an even keel and I actually felt things were going better than they had been in a long time. Some punches always come as a shock.

The room is sloping around the edges and I feel slightly seasick.

"Are you all right?"

When I nod, it feels like I'm sitting in a washing machine.

"Can you get up?"

Of course I can get up. Just not right now. All I want to do is lie here. A little bit longer.

"I didn't mean to."

Of course he didn't mean to hit so hard. Christian flickers in front of my eyes. As if he was on a badly tuned TV.

I like Christian. I like everyone at the gym. Wouldn't surprise me if they liked me too.

"Just give him a bit of time."

It's the coach talking. The one who says it's all about believing you can move mountains. That I can be as good as I want to be. And I believe him when he says it. Even though I don't necessarily believe it as much in the evening. Or the next morning. Or at school. And perhaps especially not when I'm lying here and feeling sick.

The coach and Christian help me up. I'm standing on my own two feet again.

"Take a break, why don't you," the coach says.

I don't dare to nod. Just head off toward a bench and sit there until the world has stopped tumbling and spinning and shaking.

"Boxing's not about how many times you're knocked down, but how many times you get up again," the coach tells us as he takes off my headguard and gives me an ice pack.

"I'm sure," I reply. "But I think I'll stop for now, all the same."

"See you on Wednesday, then?"

"Of course."

Christian pats me on the shoulder. If it wasn't that he lived on the other side of town, we'd probably hang out together after school.

On my way home, I feel the pain around my eye. But pain passes and I can still see. I put on my headphones and turn up the music, and the next moment everything is forgotten.

I like quite a lot of weird things, really. Like pancakes and bacon. A glass of ice-cold milk in the middle of the night. A shooting star in the sky that isn't a plane or a UFO. Or swimming on a warm summer's day when everyone else has gone home.

And I like it when Mom whispers something nice and her lips tickle my ear. I think she used to do it more before.

But there's something that beats it all. Something that makes me warm inside. A bit like someone's turned on an oven full blast in my belly.

And that's singing. Not the sort that blares out of the radio and iPods of people in my class. I like the kind of voice that makes glass shatter and fills your ears to bursting. Sometimes I forget myself and sing at full volume when I'm walking down the street. Which is a bit embarrassing. And a bit cool.

I live in an old building that could have looked newer. There are often people on the stairs, but if you don't think about it, you don't really notice them.

Mom isn't at home, so I sit down with a couple of slices of bread and do my homework. The doorbell rings, and Mom's words echo in my head: *You must never open the door unless it's someone you know.* Through the peephole, I see a man in work clothes holding up an ID card. It says *Hafslund Utilities* on the card, and there's a picture of a face that looks a bit like the man in work clothes.

He rings the bell again. Then he knocks on the door. He's probably precisely the sort of person I shouldn't open the door for. But he's got an ID card in hard plastic and looks so official that my curiosity gets the better of me.

"Is Linda Narum at home?" he asks through the gap created by the safety chain.

"No, my mom's just gone out."

"I'm sorry, but I've come to disconnect the electricity."

Mom does get behind with the bills sometimes. It

can happen to anyone. Every day is so busy and you have to remember so many things that I'm sure it's easy to forget the bills. Luckily, I remember that I'm dying.

"You can't," I say in a very sad voice.

"Sorry, son. But I don't have a choice when the bills aren't paid."

"Don't you want me to live?"

Sometimes my voice is the saddest voice I know.

"Summer's on the way, son. You won't die."

"Yes, I will. I mean it," I say, and take deep breaths, as if it's hard for me to get enough air. "At night, I sleep in an oxygen tent to help me breathe. And it won't work without electricity."

The man looks at me.

"An oxygen tent?" he repeats.

"I've got a lung disease. Do you want to see the tent?"

I tense my throat so there's a whistling sound when I breathe in.

"No, no, it's all right. I . . . well, I don't need to cut the electricity today, then. But your mom has to start paying the bills."

"She's probably just forgotten."

"For over a year?"

I shrug. The more I say, the easier it'll be to get caught

up in ridiculous lies. So I don't answer, just look at the man with hound-dog eyes.

"I'll be back."

"It was nice of you to come by."

Once I've closed the door, I have to take a deep breath. Because I don't have a tent. I'm not going to die. And I don't normally lie, at least not every day.

The world is full of white lies: someone's got bad hair, wearing strange clothes, or acting stupid, but you don't tell them that to their face. At least, I don't. I keep my mouth shut. I quite often keep my mouth very shut.

No electricity would be like staying in a cabin, every day. Or living in the Bronze Age. Best not to say anything about it to Mom. She gets upset so easily.

It's actually nice being at home alone, when you live like us. I watch a bit of TV before going to bed.

The disadvantage of finding it easy to fall asleep is that I wake up easily as well. Suddenly Mom's sitting on the edge of the bed, saying something I don't understand.

"What did you say?" I mumble.

"Hello, lovely boy," Mom says, and gives me a hug. "You're so lovely. So very lovely."

"You too, Mom."

We give each other a good, long hug. Mom likes me.

She really does. And I like her too. Mom tells me over and over how lovely I am. After a while, she lies down on the floor. Then I help her up onto the sofa and put a blanket over her.

"You're so lovely, my lovely boy," is the last thing she whispers before she falls asleep.

Outside somewhere there's an amazing shooting star. I'm sure of it.

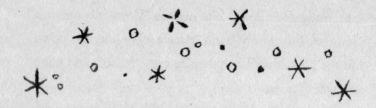

My second chapter

When I wake up, Mom is lying on her back with her mouth open. The blanket has fallen down onto the floor.

I try to get out of bed to pick it up. The first thing I register is that my eye hurts. Not much, but enough to make me not want to blink. Fortunately the room doesn't spin when I finally manage to stagger to my feet, and I tuck the blanket around Mom without waking her.

I make my own breakfast today. I don't do it every day. Sometimes Mom makes an omelet and talks so much that I stop listening. Whatever, I do like to let my thoughts go wandering before the day takes over.

Luckily there's just enough bread for breakfast and my packed lunch. I write a note for Mom: *Hope you've had a good, long sleep. We need some food. I'm happy to go to the store after school. Love you. From Bart.*

Yep, I'm called Bart. Not like the English Bart with a long *a*. No, the way people pronounce it around here sounds more like Burt, even if I was named after the little yellow guy in *The Simpsons*. Not that Mom and I watch *The Simpsons* all day, though we do sometimes, as the TV is on almost constantly. Every time, Mom tells me that she gave me that name so I'd be a funny wise guy who'd get by in life.

"But Bart's only ten," I say.

"He'll be thirteen soon as well."

"No, he won't. He's ten every single year."

I think Mom wants a son who's a bit tougher. That's why I go to boxing. *You'll thank me for it later in life,* Mom always says.

Not that I've got any plans to become a thug, but someone might try to pulp me. And then I might thank Mom. Depending on who wins.

But I'm no Bart Simpson. I should probably have been called something else, but it's a bit late now.

It takes me nine and a half minutes to get to school. And today I have eleven.

I stand in front of the school gate and take a deep

breath before the bell goes off. *New day, new possibilities*, that's what they say. Not everyone who thinks up these sayings knows what they're talking about, but I suppose this one's right. The good thing about life is that you never know what might happen. A bit like every day is a present. Unwrap it and see what's inside. I just need a little extra oxygen before going into the playground. You can't look forward to everything in life.

Now everyone will be thinking that I get bullied. Well, they're wrong.

I don't have any nicknames. No one hides my pencil case or puts my head down the toilet. It's not me they make jokes about.

Because Bertram is in my class. Yep, he's pretty unlucky with his name too. I try to distance myself from Bertram. *Bart and Bertram* doesn't exactly sound like two friends, more like a couple of clowns.

Bertram gets bullied. Not that the others give him noogies all the time or hold him out the window by the waistband of his jeans, or anything like that. Just little jibes that the teachers don't notice. A smarting insult, an outstretched leg when no one's looking, and a missing pencil case. Bertram never tells. He just stays out in the cold and wonders what he's done wrong.

I don't know.

I'd like to help Bertram become more popular, but I'm probably the last person who can fix it.

I head straight for my gang. We stand in a small circle and talk about what we've seen on TV or found on the Internet.

"You get a thumping?" one of the others in the circle asks, looking at my eye.

"Accident with the sofa," I reply.

Now, you'd think that someone might follow that up with *Did it attack you?* Or *Did the sofa die?*

But no. We're not that sort of friends.

No one at school knows that I do boxing. No one at school knows much about me. Once when we had to talk about our hobby in front of the class, I said that I collected photos of mass murderers. It's not true, but it's the kind of thing that gets everyone to shut up. If I'd told them about the boxing, you can bet that someone would try to check out my skills in the next break.

We sit in pairs in the classroom and I've been lucky for quite a few weeks now. Ada sits beside me. She's possibly the nicest girl in the class, at least one of the top three. Ada's smile is full of teeth. They're as white as fresh snow.

So now someone probably thinks that I'm in love

with Ada. You only need to say something nice about a girl, and everyone immediately imagines kissing and groping. Well, you can just turn off your fantasies. I'm not going to get together with Ada. That's just not going to happen. I know the rules. We won't even be friends. But we can sit next to each other in class. I'm not the one who made the rules.

"Hi," I say to Ada.

"Hi, Bart."

The only thing I don't really like about her is that she uses my name a lot. *Bart* sounds like a square stone in her mouth.

"I printed this out for you," she says, and hands me a copy of an article from the Internet about a guy with very bushy eyebrows.

Joe Henderson is his name. And he's killed at least four women. Maybe as many as ten. It's not the first time she's given me pictures for my collection of mass murderers.

"Cool. I haven't got him."

I need to keep some kind of list of the mass murderers she's given me, so I put them in a separate envelope with her name on it. It's under the mattress at home. There'll be a bit of explaining to do if Mom finds it, but then, I change the bed.

I put the picture in my bag. Ada's hobby is dancing. But she won't be getting any new tights from me.

So now everyone's thinking that Ada's interested in me, because she gives me pictures of mass murderers. But no, Ada already has a boyfriend. She's talked about him loads of times. He lives in a town I can't remember the name of, but it's where they've got a cabin. And he's in high school.

"I didn't understand the math homework," Ada says.

There you have it. I suppose that's the reason she gives me pictures of mass murderers.

"You can look at mine," I say, and pass her my exercise book.

She's quick at copying it.

"Thanks, Bart."

The teacher is a wirehaired growler called Egil. Apparently he was once Norway's mini-golf champion. He's standing up by his desk with a piece of paper in his hand and seems to be more lively than usual.

"Okay, settle down. I've got an important announcement."

Some of the boys sitting in the row by the window keep on chatting.

"Pay attention, boys. I want you all to listen carefully. Now, as you know, our class has been chosen for the entertainment at the end-of-year show. Our aim has to be that we're better than all previous years. Last year was catastrophic, after all. We can do better than that! We have to beat Class B, at least. So, anyone who can do something, sign up—then we can put together a suitably fantastic program. Don't be shy now."

"I'm going to dance," Ada whispers to me.

"Great," I reply.

"I'll hang the list up over here, so you can sign up," the teacher continues. "Look, see what a nice color the paper is."

There are not many things I can be certain of in this life, but here's one of them: I am not going to be doing anything in the end-of-year show.

The rest of the hour is consumed by world history, another boring one. It's in the breaks that things happen.

Sometimes I stand out on the edge of the edge. It's not always easy to say how I end up there, but I'm lost in my own thoughts and then suddenly there I am standing right down by the fence. Which is Bertram's territory. I do a quick recon to see if he's hanging around nearby but can't see him. So I hurry back to my circle and discover that they're talking about the end-of-year show.

Seems like everyone wants to take part. As if the

highway to fame and fortune starts with success in the summer show.

"Are you going to do anything, then, Bart?" one of them suddenly asks.

I should of course use his name. But to be honest, I can't remember it. Some would say that you should remember your friends' names. They've got a point.

But let me be honest: We're not the kind of friends who help each other and do fun things together after school. This is a circle for those who aren't in the in-crowd. As long as we stand in a circle talking, then we're not on the outside. I've christened the circle "No Man's Land," though I've never said it out loud.

I'm sure that the others have lots of great qualities. I just don't know enough about them. If one of them died in a terrible accident, I'd be sad, but I wouldn't break down. There's plenty else to worry about in my life. I'll maybe talk about it later, but not right now. Because right now, they're all waiting for my answer.

"Eh, no," I say.

No one asks why I don't want to. No one asks me to join in some crazy idea. They just nod and keep talking. There's going to be music, juggling, and yo-yo tricks. It could be a good end-of-year show.

The school day is like most others. No great troughs, no soaring highs. My pants tear in the crease by the crotch during break, but no one sees it. Does it count if no one notices?

On the way home from school, Ada pops up beside me just as I'm putting on my headphones. Which is a bit odd, since she doesn't live in my neighborhood. I don't know where she lives, but I've never met her on the way home from school before.

"Your pants all right?"

"Which pants? These? Is there something wrong with them?"

"Forget it. What are you listening to?" she asks, and indicates my headphones.

"A bit of everything."

"Cool. I like a bit of everything too."

"Different is good."

"Is it very different?"

"More different than normal, in this case."

"Cool. Can I have a listen . . . to some of the different stuff? Just to hear how different it is."

"Yes . . . of course."

Challenges should be faced head-on. She wants to

test my taste in music. To be honest, I don't really know how to deal with this.

I've got a pretty crappy MP3 player in my pocket. It's full of big men who sing for opera lovers and probably sound quite similar. I don't think that *different* for Ada includes people who can make windowpanes vibrate with their voice alone.

"Oh, my battery's almost dead," I say, looking down into my pocket.

"Just enough for me to hear, maybe?"

Who else my age listens to opera? No one, obviously. Okay, I admit that a lot of opera is pretty hard work. They don't have the catchiest tunes and there's a lot about death. But I love the voices. Baritones that suck me in and make my ears sweat. Well-oiled vocal cords, great lungs, and lots of stomach muscle—and suddenly the most amazing sound pours out.

Do I have any choice?

I look through the tracks. I should of course have included a couple of *Pop Idol* winners and some artists from the Disney Channel, but it's a bit late now. I press on Bryn Terfel. A Welsh ox who sings better than anyone I've heard.

When Ada takes the headphones, I realize that the

cord should be longer. We'll have to walk far too close together.

It's actually only a medium-size catastrophe if she spreads the rumor that I love opera at school. It won't make me any more popular, just more weird. Combined with the photos of mass murderers, I'm starting to match some of the real weirdos. My aim is to be gray, but I find getting the balance quite hard.

She turns to me. I expect her to have a shocked expression. Or a scornful one. To ask if I'm making fun of her.

"Cool."

"What did you say?"

"COOL!" she repeats too loudly.

I nod. Does she really mean it? She listens for a while before she takes off the headphones.

"He's got some voice," she says, then asks: "Have you got any other music on your player?"

Here goes. Why couldn't I just have downloaded some Lady Gaga, in case of a crisis.

"Maybe . . ."

"Or do you just like that kind of music?"

"No, I like loads of different stuff. But sometimes it's . . . well, it's just good . . . like that. Sometimes, not very often, though."

"You only like music like that, don't you?"

That's the problem with girls. They know things, even when you tell them something else. It's fascinating and terrifying at the same time.

"Yes, I suppose so."

"Do you sing yourself?" she asks.

Now I really am scared. I don't know how girls do it, but every time I move a muscle in my face or open my mouth, it's as if they've read long articles about me.

"I . . . I sing a bit."

It's like my mouth is doing the total opposite of what my brain is thinking. Because that's exactly what I was never going to tell anybody. And in an uncomfortable way, it feels as though Ada already knew.

"That's really cool."

"Is it?"

"I mean, what do the others do? Soccer and the school band. Do you know how many of the girls do dancing? Nearly all of them! But you, you sing opera."

"I'm not particularly good . . ."

"That doesn't matter."

I feel a bit breathless, even though we're walking really slowly.

"Can I hear you sing?"

I'm confused, I think. Does she mean it?

"It's just . . . ," I start, and look around.

I can't sing outside. Is that a good-enough excuse? Or should I say that I've got a sore throat?

Ada's not stupid. And did I say that she's got too many teeth in her mouth when she smiles?

"I'll do a recording for you. I sing best when there's music," I tell her.

And that's the truth.

"Okay. Look forward to hearing it."

"I can do it this evening."

"Great. I live just over there," she says, and points back toward the school.

I nod and make a clumsy gesture with my hand.

"You should smile more. You've got a nice smile."

Ada walks away. I stay standing where I am. What does she mean by that? Have I got a nice smile? Do girls say things like that to boys without meaning a thousand things that I don't understand? I smile at myself in the mirror too rarely to have an opinion.

And how do I look, otherwise? Well, I'm relatively small. Not really small, but another six or seven inches wouldn't go amiss. My hair's brown and quite short, and Mom cuts my hair. I've got blue eyes, but not like the sea or the sky, more like worn jeans.

I actually suspect that I look pretty anonymous. Someone you forget the minute your eyes change focus. Maybe it would have been better to have a long nose or buck teeth, something that people could remember. I could always get a snake tattoo that slithers up my neck, when I'm older. Even though that's not particularly nice.

I take a deep breath and head home. You see, sometimes I have to take a deep breath before going home, too.

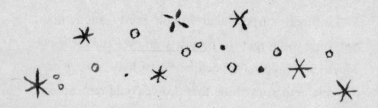

My third chapter

"What happened to your beautiful face?"

Mom examines my eye.

"Training," I explain.

"Really? That's my boy."

She strokes my hair. Mom is wearing a robe that should have been bigger.

"Go on, you give them a beating," she says, and smiles.

"I do sometimes."

"You're a born fighter, my boy."

I don't quite know what to say to that, so I just smile instead. And then she always smiles back. It doesn't matter that she's missing a tooth on her lower jaw.

I should maybe describe Mom, and our home, now

that I've explained what I look like. But sometimes it's hard to find the right words. Mom is as soft as a cushion, and the apartment is slightly smaller than a palace. Will that do?

"I've got a late shift at the supermarket tonight," Mom tells me.

"Good."

Sometimes, when Mom does extra shifts at the store, she comes back with food that's passed its sell-by date. Not that long ago, she came back with pork chops and frankfurters, and we ate so much that we just about burst. The only thing is, I don't know how to get her to work more.

"I haven't got anything for supper today. Maybe you could have some pretzel sticks," Mom says.

"I'm not really that hungry."

"Sorry that I haven't got anything else."

"I'll maybe eat some pretzels."

I'm not saying that I don't like pretzel sticks, because they're actually quite nice. But it's hard to get full on them. They're very salty and full of air. And I generally get a sore stomach before I'm full.

"I promise I'll bring a treat back from the store," Mom says.

"I might be asleep."

"Then you can have it for breakfast."

"Very good."

Two words I say so often. *Very* and *good*. Not because everything is very good, but because if you just say *okay* or *right*, or nothing at all, it sounds so negative.

"Good that you're working again," I add.

"I'll manage it this time. I promise."

"Very good."

There, I've said it again. Maybe I should have said *Don't promise too much* or *We'll see*. But I'm not the sort who says things like that. And it would just create a bad atmosphere. And bad atmospheres seldom make the days any easier.

"Grandma's coming to see us tomorrow. We'll have to go through what we're going to say."

"Okay."

I don't mention the man from Hafslund Utilities who came to see her. But I do tell her about the end-of-year show.

"Are you going to do anything?" Mom asks.

"No."

"This time I will come."

"Very good."

"I mean it, Bart. I really will come."

"See how you feel."

"I can see how I feel. But I will come."

Mom doesn't feel comfortable at school things. I can see why. People are so different. But it might actually help if she tried, even just once. Do I want her there? That's a difficult question.

When Mom has left, I put on some music, breathe deeply, and sing some long notes. After a couple of tries, I record it on the computer. I'm not exactly a real, professional opera singer, but I do sing in tune, and I even quite impress myself when I play back the recording. Hope that doesn't sound like boasting. Sorry.

It's a shame, really, that I'll never stand on a stage. But some things in life you just have to accept.

I burn a CD and write *To Ada* on it. Then regret it and burn a new one. If I write *To Ada,* it looks like a present. And it isn't a present, it's proof. I put the CD in an envelope and leave it in my bag.

I'm not the slightest bit interested in Ada. No one must think that, least of all her. Ada's going out with this really cool guy who's in high school in some unknown town miles away.

I eat a few pretzel sticks and drink some water while

I'm doing my homework. The doorbell rings, but this time I don't open the door. I don't even look through the peephole. About time I was smart. There's another ring. I turn on my MP3 player and let the song take over.

I go to bed around eleven o'clock, but there's a kerfuffle out on the stairs, so I just lie there, wide-awake, for a while. When I finally get to sleep, Mom comes home.

"You're so lovely, my lovely boy," she says, and strokes my hair.

"Mhm," I mumble.

"I'm sorry. I was going to come straight home, but then . . . I didn't mean to."

"It's all right, Mom."

"And then I forgot the food. I put the bag under the table . . ."

"It doesn't matter."

"I'm really sorry, my friend. Oh, my sweet boy . . . you're so good . . ."

It's nice when Mom strokes my hair. Sometimes she sits on my bed stroking me for a long time. If I breathe through my mouth, I can't smell her breath. But I can't fall asleep. Because Mom won't be able to get herself onto the sofa.

"You have to lie down," I say.

"You're so good, my lovely boy," she repeats.

Once I've helped Mom over onto the sofa, I fall asleep again quickly.

When the alarm clock rings in the morning, I'm in the middle of a dream that I can't remember. But it was nice. I'm sure of that.

Mom's lying on her back and sleeping very noisily. I eat the rest of the pretzel sticks and go to school.

"Here it is," I say, and hand the envelope with the CD in it to Ada, masked by the chaos as we enter the classroom.

No one seems to have noticed.

"Thanks, Bart," she says quietly, and smiles. She puts it in her bag. "I'll listen to it when I get home."

"Don't get your hopes up."

"They're sky-high already."

Ada smiles again. I realize that she's joking. But she does it in a way that makes me confused and flustered. I let her copy my homework.

The teacher says that he's looking for more acts for the summer show, before going through a list of the people who've already signed up. Ada's going to do hip-hop with some other girls from the class. Someone is going to play the violin, and the piano, some others are going to do sketches or yoyo tricks, a couple of girls are going to sing along to the playback of a Beyoncé song, and Erik is going to pull out the magic tricks that everyone has seen him do at least a hundred times before.

"Remember that all suggestions are gratefully received," the teacher says three times.

In the break, I stand with what's-his-name. Strange that it's so hard to remember his name.

"I played this really cool game yesterday," he says.

"That's good . . ."

"I can't remember what it's called. It was a guy who . . . no, first you've got to . . . well, the intro's really cool. It starts with this kind of landscape and then this guy appears with a sword. . . . Have you played it?"

"No."

"It's really cool. I played it practically all night."

That's the kind of conversation we have. Perhaps I should be more interested in the game about a guy with a sword, but I don't really play games. Not because I don't want to.

There are probably too many voices and too much noise in the playground to say that the silence is oppressive. But I don't have much to say that can beat swordsmen and really good graphics. *You see, Mom woke me up around three to tell me that she loved me about three hundred times.* I've got a feeling that what's-his-name might have problems talking to me after that.

"It's warm today," he says.

I nod, even though it's not particularly warm today.

Then suddenly he's standing there. Bertram has snuck up beside me. Now we're a circle of three. One of them is Bertram. An alarm goes off for me and what's-his-name.

"The periodic table is quite a classification system," I say, hoping that Bertram will leave if he doesn't understand what we're talking about.

The problem is that neither does what's-his-name.

"What are you talking about?"

I should have winked when I said it.

"Forget it."

"I was just wondering . . . ," starts Bertram.

So, is he going to ask if we can be friends now? Say that as outsiders we should stick together?

"I just wondered if you wanted to do a rap with me for the end-of-year show?" he continues.

It's a question that needs time to sink in. Not because I'm in any doubt as to what my answer is, but because I'm suddenly not sure that I heard right.

What's-his-name reacts first.

"My mom won't let me."

"Won't let you?" Bertram asks.

I'm also interested to see how he's going to get himself out of this one.

"Yes, she doesn't want me to move to the ghetto and walk around with a gun."

His cheeks take on a pink tinge when he says it. Bertram looks at me. It must be possible to come up with a better lie than that.

"I'm going to sing on my own at the end-of-year show."

"Oh, right," Bertram says, and leaves.

"Are you going to sing at the summer show?" what's-his-name asks when Bertram's out of hearing range.

"No, but I had to think of something. My lie was better than yours."

"It wasn't a lie. My mom's obsessed with stopping me from having anything to do with rap. She thinks I'll end up on the dole then and become a criminal."

"The dole?" I say, and laugh too loud. "The dole, right."

Good thing I don't want to be an actor.

"Bertram raps. That's crazy."

"What if he becomes popular?"

Both of us freeze. If Bertram becomes a respected rapper, the others in the class will have to find a new target for all their sarcasm and pencil-case emptying. Obviously there are unwritten rules about things like that, too. The thought terrifies us both.

"Should we do something after school . . . ?" he asks abruptly.

And suddenly I remember that he's called Jonas. Maybe Jonas can be my best friend? You're not left on the outside as easily if you've got a best friend. Though obviously you have to remember your best friend's name.

The spark of hope only burns for a second. I don't know if I can be friends with anyone outside school. What would I say if he wanted to come home with me?

"I've got lots of other plans, so I don't think I can . . . Jonas."

"My name's Harald."

"I knew that."

Luckily, the bell rings. Conversations like that are a bit like skating. Suddenly you veer off to the side and fall flat on your face.

* * *

After the last class, I exit as fast as I can so there's no risk of anyone tagging along. I put my headphones over my ears and kick the player into life.

Miming along to music as you walk down the street looks a little wacko. I've nearly always turned down the volume on my voice, but mouthing along to opera probably looks like I'm trying to catch flies. At the same time, it's a good way to learn all the songs. It's a bit like my life has its own soundtrack. It's a pretty boring movie, with overdramatic music.

Mom isn't home, so I stand in the middle of the room and sing at the top of my voice. I can't call and check where she is, for two simple reasons: I've never had a cell phone, and her phone has been blocked. Mom bought the MP3 player from Cheap Charlie. He lives in the same building as us and is an expert in good deals. It was also him who sold us the computer for six hundred kroner. He said it was so cheap because he'd bought a new one.

There were loads of pictures on the computer and none of them were of Cheap Charlie. A policeman who came to school once said that fencing was the same as stealing. In which case, we paid six hundred kroner to be thieves. *Those people can afford to buy a new PC*, Mom said when we looked through the photos. They'd been on vacation to loads of warm places, and they had a huge trampoline in their backyard. But still, it's not fun to lose all your pictures, so I burned them onto some CDs, found the address on a letter that had been scanned in, and sent them the pictures in the mail. I mean, they might have had a backup, but you never know.

I made sure to wipe off any fingerprints from the CDs and envelope. Prison's not a place for my mom, and I don't want to find out what kind of living conditions Social Services have to offer.

I hook up to the neighbor's open network and go onto Facebook. My friends total four boys from boxing and two *Simpsons* fans. Nothing much exciting happens in their lives and I never post updates.

Then I search for Dad. As usual, I get just over 86 million hits. The chances are fairly big that some of them are about Dad. Only I don't know which. Dad is American and his name is John Jones. That's about all Mom will say. I'm not so sure that she knows any more herself, because they didn't really have time to get to know each other. Some time or other I'm going to find him and ask him to take me to Universal Studios and four or five other theme parks. But for the moment, I don't have much to go on. None of the John Joneses I've found pictures of look anything like me. There are about a hundred John Joneses on Wikipedia and a lot of them are dead.

And I don't discover a John Jones who's looking for his unknown son in Norway today either. Luckily I've got a few million Web pages left.

Mom's out of breath when she comes home, with my grandmother in tow.

"Hello, love," Grandma says, and gives me a hug that smells of attics and nicotine.

"Hello," I say with my mouth full of blouse.

"I'm so glad that you're going to sing for me today," she exclaims.

"Am I?"

I look over at Mom.

"You need to practice singing in front of people."

Mom has heard me singing in the bathroom countless times. There's good acoustics in there. I lock the door, close my eyes, and sing as loud as I can. And it's fine, even though I know Mom's outside the door. It would make Mom happy if I sang for Grandma. And Grandma would be thrilled. Even I would be pretty pleased.

"I can try."

Grandma sits down on the sofa and tells me about the bus journey and that she won some coffee at bingo yesterday. Mom opens the bags from Burger King and puts the food onto plates. The room is filled with a delicious smell. One burger for Grandma, two for me, and six for Mom.

"So, a little song for your supper?" Mom asks, and smiles.

I close my eyes. Take a breath. Imagine that I'm in the bathroom. And then I sing.

It might just be starting problems. I mean, after all, I haven't warmed my voice up. But it just gets worse and worse. I screech like a broken loudspeaker, and every note cuts through the room like a runaway lawnmower.

A pair of curious eyes and it's as if my vocal cords get knotted and someone has poured gravel down my throat. I don't dare open my eyes to see my grandmother's sad expression. She's bound to say something nice afterward, pure lies, in the way that only well-intentioned grandmothers can lie. I stop singing and just stand in the middle of the floor in my own darkness. My voice is not intended for anyone other than me. Sorry.

I open my eyes. No one claps.

"Good, Bart," Grandma says. "Now, I'm hungry."

Instead of becoming stuck in a bog of lies, Grandma moves on.

"Those burgers look good," she says with enthusiasm. I've got a smart grandmother.

Of course I've dreamed about standing onstage and soaking up the applause and jubilation. The feeling is presumably better than fantastic. But it's not going to happen. The good thing about me is that I just accept that not everything works out in this life. Only idiots believe that everything turns out well.

What I hope is not going to happen, happens as soon as we start supper. Grandma asks about Mom's job at Telenor. There's a lot that's good about the job. She's making her way up the ladder. At least, that's what Mom and I have agreed. I've googled *Service Level Manager* several times to find out what they do. But the English words that explain it are not ones we learn at school, and Google Translate doesn't always make sense. But I've written down some words on a piece of paper.

Mom tells a story about a colleague who dressed up as a cell phone for a party. I don't think Grandma fully understands it either.

"Evidently Mom's really good at analyzing voice flows," I offer as soon as Mom's finished the story.

Mom and Grandma look at me. I look down at the piece of paper.

"Yesterday you said something about investigating proactive people being more fun than securing customer complaints."

Grandma sends Mom a questioning look, and for a moment I think it looks like she's smiling. Mom looks at me like I was something stuck to the bottom of her shoe.

"I don't think he quite understands," Mom says.

"Well, it's good that you've got a job like that, at least," Grandma says, then adds: "Even if you don't have any qualifications."

She looks over at me with the same strange expression.

"I'm really proud of her," I add.

If Mom had just checked on the Internet, we could have agreed what she did at work. Does Grandma really believe that she does *level servicing* and manages four people, and that two of them are called Alf?

"Does that mean you'll be moving soon, then?" Grandma asks.

"Yes, we're moving," Mom says.

There's often an odd tone to Grandma's questions. As if she's a bit sad when she asks them. Mom asks us to keep eating while the burgers are still warm.

Grandma talks about her nice neighbors while we eat. I drop out of the conversation and look forward to Grandma leaving, so I can sing in the bathroom. After we've eaten, I surf the Internet to find something about singers who can't sing for anyone except themselves. I find a story about the Philippine authorities that fine people for singing the national anthem out of tune, but nothing to help me. So I play a game instead to pass the time.

"Mom told me about the end-of-year show. I'm coming, as Mom has to work late," Grandma says before she goes.

"Very good," I say.

Grandma always comes to things at school. She never asks why Mom always works late when there's something at school.

"Do you need anything?" Grandma asks as she stands at the door.

"No, we've got everything we need," Mom assures her.

"Maybe I could give Bart a hundred kroner, for something special?"

"There's no need, really. He's just gotten his pocket money."

"You've got something on your shoe," I say, and point to some dirty paper tissue that's stuck to the sole of her shoe.

"Oh, it's probably something I took in with me from the stairs . . . I mean, the street. They don't wash the streets anymore. No one cares what the town looks like anymore."

"No, it's not very good right now," Mom agrees.

When Grandma's gone, Mom has to sit down on the sofa. It's started to creak ominously.

"Jesus, that woman goes on," Mom says.

"I think she's all right."

"You'll get pocket money soon, Bart. But the welfare money doesn't come until the twentieth."

"I don't need money for anything right now."

I lock myself in the bathroom. The notes pour out like cut glass and I feel the song surging up from somewhere in the depths of my lungs and stomach. It's a bit like I'm two people: the one who damages eardrums and the one who sings and makes mothers proud. I don't think the two have ever met.

When I come out, Mom gives my back a gentle rub.

"Don't think about it," she says. "It's good to be able to sing for yourself."

"Mhm."

"And it's really nice to listen . . . through the door."

"I have to go to boxing."

"Knock 'em dead."

Flyweight. That's the class they're training me for. It might as well be called gnatweight. It's for people who weigh between 108 and 112 pounds. Right now, I weigh 80 pounds. The advantage of being so small is often that you're fast. So my coach says. One day that will surely be to my advantage too.

"Good work, Bart. Now you can do fifty sit-ups."

There's nothing wrong with the coach. He just wants me to be someone who can keep up with the other runts in flyweight. Sometimes, late at night under the comforter, I dream that I'll grow like a dandelion over the next few years and suddenly be on a level with Muhammad Ali and knock out the competition from far-flung countries. The dream makes me sweat.

"Come on, Bart. Where's the speed?"

Boxing is often called *the noble art of self-defense*. But it's actually all about knocking out your opponent.

"Good effort."

That's me. *Good effort*. I always give my all. Even though that's nearly never enough.

I do a couple rounds sparring with Christian. We're the same age, but he's still a head taller than me and has muscles that I was never given. But he's nice enough. We train well together and he never tries to floor me when the coach has his back turned.

At training, we never talk about people who've been turned into vegetables by boxing. It's all about the great fighters, heroes who have taken and given a beating and taken home prize belts that don't fit any pants.

Except for a few *eh*s in class, I don't notice any signs that I'm brain-dead.

"How's it going?" Christian asks when we're sitting on the plastic chairs by the wall.

"Okay."

"Your eye's all right again."

"Yep."

"Did anyone bother you at school?"

Apart from being friends on Facebook, I don't really know Christian. The question is a bit of an uppercut.

"Eh, no."

"Good. Because if they do, just let me know."

"Oh, right."

Quite a fascinating thought, really. Christian appearing and beating up people like August and Johnny.

The teacher always says something about pissing in your pants to keep warm. Which helps there and then, but Christian can't show up every day to give the boys a going-over.

Christian gets up and starts to hammer the punch bag. I keep myself happy with some shadow boxing.

"Have you got a minute?" the coach asks toward the end of the session.

I lope after him into the office and sit down on a worn wooden chair. There are black-and-white photos of boxers like George Foreman, Sugar Ray Leonard, and Ali, of course, on the wall. A long time ago, the coach explained to us that Ali was the greatest and would always be the greatest.

I wipe away the sweat with my arm and start to take off my boxing gloves. The coach leans back and looks at me long and hard.

"I wish everyone loved each other as much as everyone loves me. Then the world would be a better place."

I look up at the coach.

"It was Ali who said that. You know, the one who also said he would float like a butterfly and sting like a bee."

That's the coach's favorite quote. It's the last thing he says to his boxers before a fight.

"The shiner looks better."

"Yes."

"Bart, I've been thinking. Are you sure that you want to continue with the boxing?"

"I come to all the training sessions."

"You do. There's nothing wrong with your commitment. I just thought . . . well, maybe another sport would suit you better."

"Like what?"

"The possibilities are endless. Ski jumping, perhaps."

"Ski jumping?"

"Yes, you're quite thin, you see. Or something totally different. Curling."

Mom wouldn't be so enthusiastic if I started ski jumping or curling. How can I defend myself with a curling stone? It must be the coach's way of telling me that my boxing sucks from here to the moon. But I can't stop. Mom couldn't take that.

"Has Mom not paid?" I ask.

"Yes, she has. Absolutely."

"But wasn't it Muhammad Ali who said that a person who doesn't dare in this life will never achieve anything?" I wonder.

"Eh, yes, perhaps it was," my coach replies.

"Well, then I can't give up now."

"That's a very good attitude. But boxing is a sport where you actually have to punch people."

"And?" I say, pretending that I don't know where this is going.

"And you don't punch."

"But I'm a good guard."

"That's great. But you do have to punch sometimes."

"What if . . . if I start doing it soon?"

"Obviously, that would be an advantage. So you don't want to think about anything else? Handball's supposed to be fun."

"I like boxing."

"That's good. It's a good sport. I'm really happy that you like boxing."

Coaches are supposed to make you good. Not encourage you to take up another sport. I almost tell him that.

"Great. So we're agreed, then," I say instead.

"And you'll start punching soon?"

"Yeah, any day now."

I leave the office and go to the changing room. Of course I know he's right. A fight where one of the opponents doesn't even try to punch would be totally unequal. But the coach once told us about a fight between Muhammad Ali and George Foreman some-where in Africa. Ali wore Foreman out by dancing around the ring and avoiding his opponent's punches. When Foreman was completely exhausted, Ali took his aim and nearly punched him out of the ring.

I'm probably not quite there yet. But I will be.

I believe.

Mom stays at home in the evening and we watch a documentary on TVNorge about the tallest woman in the world. She lives in China and lies in bed most of the day. Which doesn't exactly make you happy.

When I go to bed, I think that it was a bad idea to give Ada the CD. She should at least have signed an agreement that no one else would be allowed to hear it. I get so annoyed with myself that I lie there awake until Mom falls asleep with the TV on. Once I've turned it off, I lie there and listen to the sawmill in her mouth. An unease starts to grow somewhere deep down inside me. As if I've done something without having any idea of the consequences.

And I fall asleep before I have time to think about shooting stars that aren't airplanes or UFOs.

My fourth chapter

Mom got up at the same time as me. She made pancakes for breakfast. It's been a long time since she's done that. It doesn't matter that we're out of sugar and syrup. Because we've got bacon. It crunches nicely when I chew.

"Here's twenty kroner for your lunch," Mom says, and presses the coin into my hand.

I've explained to her plenty of times that the school doesn't sell lunches and no one is allowed to leave the playground. But it's the thought that counts.

"Thank you, will do."

At school, Ada comes over before the bell's even rung.

"Is it really you singing?"

That actually gives me an unexpected opportunity to lie my way out of everything. To say that it was something that I found on the Internet. Scrape the ground with the tip of my shoe and admit that I did it to impress her. Maybe laugh it off and just ask if she really thought it was me.

But then there's a glow about her.

"Yes, it's . . . me."

"You should perform at the summer show!"

I had actually guessed that she might suggest this. And I had thought hard about which illnesses and excuses might stop people from asking. But somehow I can't bring myself to say any of it to Ada. I don't know that *want* is a good-enough reason, but it's the best half truth I can think of.

"I don't want to."

"Of course you should. Everyone will be super impressed."

"I would appreciate it if you didn't say to anyone that I don't want to."

"Can't even I convince you?" she asks with a smile.

For a fraction of a second, it's tempting to say, *Yeah, since it's you who's asking and you're smiling with all your teeth, I'll do it.* But that's not going to happen. It would be a disaster and Ada would never talk to me again. I shake my head.

"Sorry. Can I get the CD back?"

"I'd like to listen to it again."

"But you won't play it for anyone, will you?"

"But it's so good. And no, I won't."

"I have to play it for my grandmother, you see."

I don't know whether that's a lie or not. Maybe I should, so that Grandma realizes that I can do more than just pollute her ears.

We stand there on the playground. Why hasn't the bell rung yet? No Man's Land is standing some way off, looking in my direction. Ada waves to some friends, but they don't come over. Should she really be standing here with me?

"Will you sing for me sometime, maybe?" she asks suddenly.

"Take some earplugs."

"You're funny, Bart."

"Might be better if you came with me to boxing one day."

Ada bursts out laughing.

"You do boxing. Yeah, right. I can just picture it."

I have no intention of convincing Ada that I do

boxing, but I do wish she wouldn't laugh so hard.

She starts to tell me that Lise in our class has secretly dated someone who does boxing. But I mustn't tell anyone. Why is she telling me this? Then she says that Lise likes boys with muscles. But apparently that's a secret too.

Finally the bell rings and we head toward the classroom. The anxiety in my stomach has caught fire and someone keeps fueling it with paper and dry wood.

I couldn't even begin to tell you what we did in the next class. My brain was miles away and didn't return until the bell rang again. I like taking a vacation during class, but it does mean that I have to work harder on the homework.

We're going to practice for the summer show in the next class. Anyone who's not taking part has to do PE instead. I put on my sneakers.

During break, after a couple of games of dodgeball, I register that something's different. It feels like I've suddenly gone Day-Glo or have got eczema. A couple of the cool guys nod to me, like we're old friends.

Something's changed during the PE class, and it's got nothing to do with my dodgeball skills.

I notice Ada. She looks really upset. Like she's done

something I've asked her not to do. Fear squeezes my bones.

We go back into the classroom, and when I ask how the rehearsals went, she replies without looking at me: "Good."

Ada has long, dark blond hair and a nose that's straight as a ruler. Her eyes are as brown as the teacher's leather bag and her smile would melt ice. But that smile is very well hidden right now.

The teacher comes in and immediately starts to talk passionately about the end-of-year show. There's no end to how impressed he is with Class A. They've got rising stars in several categories.

"It's fantastic that so many of you have already signed up," he says, then pauses. "But I also want to say that modesty is a sign of quality. We can all feel unsure as to whether we're good enough or not. But if you've got talent, it's actually not that easy to keep it under wraps. Talent has a power of its own. Sooner or later, it will out."

He pauses again. I realize he's looking at me. And his look tells me more than those stupid words.

"Bart," he continues. "I really want you to sing in the summer show."

Everyone stares at me. I look over at Ada. She looks down at her desk.

I understand that the teacher wants to put together the best possible program so he can brag about it in the staff room at lunch for the next six months. The others want to crush Class B.

It's impossible not to lie at moments like this. I should really have prepared an answer that would just trip off my tongue before the teacher even finished speaking.

"Eh," I start, trying desperately to formulate the words that don't seem to want to go together. "Eh, it won't really work."

The truth is that I haven't given a moment's thought to what I might say in an emergency like this. *It won't really work?* What is it I'm doing instead? Visiting the king?

The teacher looks pensively at the ceiling and carries on: "I want . . . I mean, we would really like you to close the show. You sing really . . . I have to say, I'm impressed, Bart."

Ada is still studying a stain on the top of the desk. There must be a magic sentence that can get me out of this.

I think so hard my brain hurts. Searching for words

other than *no*. That word is all I want to say now, loud and clear with an exclamation mark to finish.

"I can . . . I suppose . . . do it," I say eventually.

"Fantastic! That's wonderful, Bart. That's made me very happy."

Don't suppose he'll be quite as happy when I've done the finale and ruined everything.

The teacher carries on saying how pleased he is with Class A. The school was founded in 1910 and the teacher has only been working here for three years, but he knows all the same that this will be the best show in the school's history. We will definitely be better than Class B.

It's kind of weird, but I'm not angry with Ada, even though I should be. I'm actually more annoyed with myself for not being angry.

In the break, people come up to me who I can't remember ever speaking to.

"The teacher played your recording to everyone," says August, who's one of the ones who most often gives Bertram an extra shove. "You're pretty awesome."

"I don't know."

"We're going to thrash Class B."

Why does everything have to be a competition?

Can't we just do our best and hope that people like it? I have to keep questions like that locked up in my head. If I said them out loud, I'd probably get a thrashing myself.

Obviously, I can't actually sing at the end-of-year show. But you can't just say that you're ill or you've lost your voice. Maybe kidnapping or ending up in the hospital will do the trick. But I'm not so sure.

"What do you think the answer is, Bart?" the teacher asks from the front of the room in the next class.

"Um," I start. I have no idea what subject we're doing. "I was thinking about singing and things like that," I tell him.

"That's fine, Bart. Absolutely fine. You just carry on. I'll ask someone else."

Talk about giving yourself a knockout punch.

I'm the first person out of the classroom after the last class.

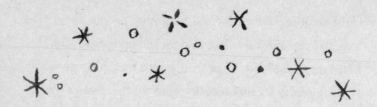

My fifth chapter

Something crunches under my shoes as I walk up the stairs. The sound makes me shudder. If I was going to do something horrible and illegal, I would do it somewhere where no one could see. No one seems to think like that in our building. So something crunches under my shoes in the hall. But it doesn't cut me.

A small man comes veering down the stairs and I hug the wall to avoid a collision.

I let myself into the apartment. Mom's watching TV. "There's my boy," she says, and waves me over.

I get a hug that squeezes the air out of me. Mom is the nicest person I know. She's quite strong as well. It makes me feel fuzzy inside when I think things like that.

"I'm going to do my homework," I say.

"You're going to be something great one day. I know it."

"And if I don't turn out to be great?"

"You're going to be something great. I just know it."

The doorbell rings. We're not expecting anyone.

"Geir!" a man's voice shouts. Wouldn't surprise me if it was the one who passed me in the hall. "Open the door, for crissake!"

Neither Mom nor I have ever been called Geir.

Mom goes over to the door and calls from inside: "You've got the wrong apartment. Geir doesn't live here."

"Come on, Geir."

"There's no one called Geir here."

There's silence outside. Then he hammers on the door again.

"What've you done with Geir?"

The door starts to vibrate alarmingly. All the doors in the building are identical and not particularly solid. Sometimes at night you hear someone standing out there wondering why the key doesn't work. When I think about it, that happens quite a lot during the day too.

"No one's done anything with Geir. He just doesn't live here," Mom explains.

"Geir! You owe me money!" the man outside shouts, and keeps knocking.

You wouldn't need to be a weightlifter to break down the door, so it doesn't help trying to drown out the noise with an MP3 player. We have to get the guy to stop.

I go over to the door and say loudly: "Geir is dead!"

He stops knocking.

"Huh? Geir's dead? You know what, thought he might be 'cause I haven't seen him in ages. That's crazy, I mean, that I thought that, like. I mean, sorry for bothering you. Are you his son?"

"Eh, yes."

"Sorry. Won't bother you again. Too bad about your dad, I mean. That's crazy."

He carries on talking for a while, but his voice gets quieter and quieter and soon it's hard to hear what he's saying. I've no idea who Geir is, and have no plans to be his son.

"Smart," Mom says, and asks if I want a doughnut.

It turns out that Mom's been to the store and bought Coke, chips, and a dozen doughnuts, but forgotten to buy supper.

"I can go down to the store again," I say. "We could

have sausages or meatballs, or something simple like that. Maybe with some potatoes."

"Yes, why don't you?" Mom says. "Good idea, Bart."

She goes back to watching TV; it's a repeat of some reality show. I start to put my shoes on, but stop before I tie the laces.

"But maybe you've got no money?" I say. The twenty kroner she gave me won't buy supper.

Mom looks at me. She's got icing all around her mouth.

"I'll be getting more money soon. Very soon. Then you'll get pocket money."

"It's fine. I can have a doughnut, it's all right."

I take off my shoes and start to do my homework while I eat a doughnut with pink icing.

Just the thought of standing in front of all those serious faces and the big stage makes the notes jangle, even though I'm locked in the bathroom.

"Is everything okay?" Mom asks in a worried voice when I come out.

"Just got something in my throat."

"Oh, it's horrible getting something caught in your throat."

"I'm sure I'll get it out."

"It normally sorts itself out. Still hungry?"

There's one solitary doughnut with white icing left. My stomach screams no, but Mom holds it out to me and I don't want her to ask again if something's wrong.

"Thanks. Looks tempting."

Just then the doorbell rings again. I've suggested that we should paint the door yellow so people stop getting the wrong door. But Mom's scared we'll get thrown out.

Presumably it's Geir's friend who's forgotten that Geir's dead. Mom and I pretend not to notice when there's another ring on the bell. The doughnut is a mass of sweet dough swelling in my mouth.

"It's Ada," a voice says outside the door.

I'm sure there are greater shocks in life. But right now I can't think what they might be. I'm shell-shocked and promptly give up any attempt to get my act together.

"Bart? Are you there?" Ada asks.

"Is it someone you know?" Mom whispers.

"No," I say.

"But she said your name."

"Well, I mean . . . yes, but . . ."

"Bart, can't you just open the door?" Ada says in a loud voice.

"I think you're going to have to let her in," Mom says.

"I'm sure she'll go away eventually."

I look over at the door. Ada is standing behind it. She's come up the stairs and down the hall. Things have crunched under her feet. She'll have looked down and seen the used needles and other trash. Maybe she's bumped into some of the neighbors. Someone stumbling on the stairs or staggering down the hall. Maybe someone with knees that don't work and the world's smallest pupils down by the mailboxes.

It's actually all right living in public housing as long as no one at school knows. But now it's out of the bag. Untrustworthy Ada is standing outside my door. What's she doing here?

"Who is she?" Mom whispers.

"No one."

"Well, obviously she's not. She knows your name."

"Someone in my class."

"Someone in your class? Who's come here?"

"She might go away soon."

"I can hear you whispering in there," Ada informs us from outside.

Mom gets up and opens the door.

"Hi, I'm Bart's mom," she says, holding out her hand. "Linda. Why don't you come in?"

I can see how Ada looks at Mom, then takes in the view of the apartment. Mom moves to one side and Ada steps in gingerly. I guess I should have described our place a long time ago. But somehow it didn't seem like the right time. We don't live in one of those apartments that a real estate agent would call desirable. In fact, it can hardly be called an apartment. Mom and I live in one room. I sleep on a sofa bed and Mom sleeps on the normal sofa. There are piles of magazines and papers and stuff on the floor, but you can see some of the linoleum in the middle of the floor. We've got a bookshelf full of anything but books and a fridge that's a bit too warm. One wall is pale yellow; the others are white and show the marks of where pictures once hung. We need curtains, but there are other things we need to buy first. We've got a list somewhere. It's quite long.

Mom and I live here. We've never had a visit from anyone in the class before. And now Ada is standing in the middle of the room and the apartment feels smaller and more cramped than ever. Mom tidies away the sheets and blankets on the sofa.

"Sit down. I was just about to go shopping," she says.

"But you haven't . . . ," I start saying, and then suddenly stop.

"It's fine," Mom says. "Why don't you get Ada a glass of juice or something, Bart?"

I nod. I finished the juice yesterday.

Neither Ada nor I say anything until Mom has gone out the door. I attempt a smile, but don't know that I succeed.

"Your mom is—"

"I know," I interrupt.

No matter what word she was going to say, I don't want to hear it. Beached whale. Ginormous. Superfatso. Very overweight. Back end of a bus. There's no nice way to say it. Because she's not *a little round* or *chunky*. She's much more than that.

"She's . . . nice," Ada says.

"Oh right. I guess . . . she is. How did you find me?"

"I got your address from school."

"You shouldn't have come." It just falls out of my mouth.

"I'm really sorry about what happened. Lise saw you give me the envelope and wanted to know what it was. And I just wanted us to do the best we could and the teacher was wild for it. I've never seen him like that. . . . But then I remembered what you'd said about not playing it to anyone. I thought that maybe what you really wanted was for me to play it after all. Why did you give me the recording?"

Why is she asking about things that are impossible to explain?

"I don't know."

"Whatever, I just wanted to say . . . sorry."

"It's okay. Well, it's not really. But it's nice of you to say sorry."

"Why don't you want anyone else to hear it?"

I take a deep breath.

"I can't sing for other people. Not even for you. I can only do it when I lock myself in the bathroom. That's why I had to do a recording for you."

"Because you get so nervous? Stage fright sort of thing?"

"Yes . . . or I don't know. Everything just clams up. Do you want some juice?"

"Okay."

I've already forgotten that we don't have juice.

I can't find a clean glass, so I have to wash one before I fill it with water from the tap.

"Here you go." I give it to Ada. "Sorry it's such a mess in here."

"Doesn't matter," she says, and takes a drink. "Aren't you having anything?"

To wash another glass would just show how often we do in fact wash the dishes, so I shake my head. It's not that we never clean up, we just don't do it every day.

"It's nice . . . water."

I try to think of something to say to make it less awkward. Maybe those words don't exist.

"Have you been living here long?" she asks.

Questions like that don't make things any better. She might as well ask if we've not had money for a long time, or if it's something more recent.

"We're hoping to move soon."

I'm not lying. Because I'm not saying that we *are* going to move. I'm just saying that we *hope* to move. I certainly do. I hope every single day. When I'm woken up by arguments in the middle of the night, my hope is more acute. Whenever I almost make friends at school, I hope so much that my stomach aches. And sometimes I think that Mom actually hopes even more than me.

"I'm sure it'll be good. Moving, I mean," Ada says.

"Even though it's nice here. It's not as bad as out in the hall, at least."

"Thanks."

How can you give someone like me a compliment? It's not as dirty as out in the hall. Well, it's true, if nothing else.

"I've got the CD with me," she says, and takes it out of the inner pocket of her jacket.

I put it down on the table as if it was something I don't want to dirty my hands with. Ada doesn't fit in here. I fit in. Everything about her is wrong here. I hope that she'll finish her water soon and leave. But before she does, I ask her to promise one thing: "You won't say anything to the others, will you?"

"About what?"

"About . . . here."

"How you live? Course not. I won't even say that I've been here. Why would I?"

No, why would she? That would be the same as admitting that she hangs out with people who live in slums. I really want to say to her that she's perhaps not the best person in the world at keeping secrets. That she seems to be a bit leaky.

"What are you going to do about the show?" Ada asks, interrupting my thoughts.

"Do you think playback's an option?"

"They might see through it."

"Maybe I could move to South America."

Ada bursts out laughing. Then she spots something in the mess.

"Is that . . . ?"

I try to see where she's looking.

"So you were telling the truth?" she continues. "You do boxing?"

"Yes. But mainly I get thrashed. I haven't started to punch back yet."

She laughs again. Then she looks around the room, as though she's looking for more surprises. She could have said something about us having a lot in a small space. Or wondered if the piles of paper and magazines ever toppled over. Or asked if I knew what was at the bottom. I don't know how you make small talk in an apartment like this. Whatever, I'm glad she doesn't ask any more questions.

"I should maybe go now," she says.

The strange thing is that she doesn't stand up. As if she's waiting for me to do something. I look around the room and think about what it must be like to see this chaos for the first time. I'm so used to it that it's almost as if the mess doesn't exist.

"Muhammad Ali was actually called Cassius Clay, but he changed his name when he turned Muslim," I say.

"Is that someone you know?"

"No, he was a famous boxer from way back. He's from the USA."

"Oh right, tell me more."

And so I tell her more. Even though I bet Ada isn't that interested in boxing. It turns out I know quite a lot about Muhammad Ali, because the stories just pour out of me. About him being called *The Greatest* and that his heavyweight title fights against Joe Frazier and George Foreman are legendary. He could say things about his opponents in rhyme, and I can even remember some of his quotes. She seems interested, even when I tell her about a technique he called *rope-a-dope* and that he refused to fight in the war in Vietnam, a country we've learned about at school.

When I take a break, Ada suddenly starts talking about her dancing. She does locking, jazz, and musical theater, and she describes the classes in a way that makes me say that it sounds a lot like what we do at boxing. But they don't punch each other, and no one goes home with a black eye.

Suddenly we've been talking so long that Mom

comes home, out of breath, with two huge bags of groceries. I don't know where she got the money.

"Do you want to stay for supper?" Mom asks. "We're going to have meatballs."

Ada hesitates.

"I could call and ask," she says. "Is it okay if I go out into the hall?"

"Of course."

I know why she has to go out into the hall. She has to lie. Tell her parents that she's with anyone other than weirdo Bart and his fat mother in a dirty public housing apartment. Not so hard to understand, really.

Ada is allowed to stay and have supper with her friend or whoever she told her parents it was. Mom starts to clear the table, the only table we have, which is actually too low for eating.

"How nice to get a visitor," Mom says.

Ada smiles.

The whole time we're eating, I'm terrified that Mom's going to talk about our welfare money and cheap supermarkets. Or lie about her Telenor job. But Mom only asks the usual questions and otherwise keeps her mouth shut. The meatballs are actually good, even though they're not homemade. The conversation limps on, but at least there are no silences.

"That was lovely," Ada says after the meal.

"Glad you liked the food," Mom says.

I think that's the kind of thing moms should say. After Ada has said thank you, silence sinks over the table. Mom smiles and rubs her thighs. I can't really ask Ada to my room. And Mom can't go anywhere other than the bathroom and that might seem a bit odd.

"I should really go home," Ada says suddenly.

"Yes, and I should do my homework," I say.

"It was nice having you visit," Mom adds.

"See you tomorrow, Bart."

"Yeah, see you tomorrow."

She gets up. I want to say something to make her laugh on her way out. People think they've had a good time when the last thing they do is laugh.

"Did I tell you my mom went to Kingston?"

"Jamaica?"

"No, she wanted to."

If you say something stupid, they'll just remember how stupid the whole visit was. Someone has frazzled my brain.

"Bye, Linda," Ada calls on the way out.

Mom gives her a wave from the sofa.

"Come again, whenever you like," Mom says.

I follow Ada out into the hall.

"You mustn't come again," I mutter.

"I like your mom."

We don't meet anyone on the stairs. She gives me a hug, which makes my cheeks burn even more, and I forget to say bye. Or maybe I do. For a moment it feels like some of this has never happened. That I'm living in my own little bubble. Where girls from school actually come to see me.

I follow her at a distance in case someone decides to mug her on the way out. The state of the floor by the mailboxes brings me back to reality. There are some leaflets with footprints all over them. I see the remains of a couple of dirty syringes over by the wall. There's an oven mitt and bits of an old camping chair on the stairs. I've stopped being surprised by what people leave lying around.

And then I remember the revolting paper under Grandma's shoes, and she forgot herself and said that it was probably something from the stairs, then quickly corrected herself and said the street. I think about what Ada said about the apartment at least being nicer than the hall. What sort of comparison is that? I go back up and find a blank piece of paper. As I'm writing, Mom comes over and stands behind me.

"Sorry," she says.

"For what?"

"That we live here and that . . . well, it's not always easy to have friends over."

"She won't tell anyone."

Mom pats me on the back while she reads what I've written.

Do you want to live in a trash pile? I live on the second floor and would be very happy if you could help me tidy up on Sunday at 5 p.m. It's my birthday. I'll be 13. Bart.

"It might help," I say.

"That's great. Really good. But Bart . . ."

I look up at Mom.

"What is it?" I ask.

"If we lived anywhere else, people would definitely come. But . . . I'm afraid the people who live here—"

"There's no harm in trying," I interrupt. "Will you come?"

Mom continues to rub my back.

"You know what the doctor says."

"Yes, I know."

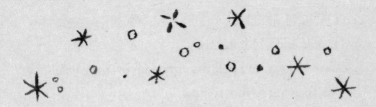

My sixth chapter

Later in the evening, Mom goes out. She promises not to be late.

I've hung two posters up in the hall. When I've finished my homework, I sing for a while. Someone knocks on the wall and it feels good. They've heard me.

Mom hasn't come back by the time I go to bed. I lie there thinking about Ada. Or to be more precise: I lie there thinking about what Ada is thinking. Hardly surprising that I can't get to sleep.

But I must have dozed off at some point, because when I open my eyes and see Mom sitting on the edge of my bed, I was in the middle of a dream about Ada, two tigers, and a shooting star.

"Oh, hi," I mumble.

"I've decided," Mom says.

"Good," I say, and pull the covers up over my head.

"We're going to move, son."

"Great . . ."

"Lovely, lovely boy. You deserve to live in a normal place with normal neighbors."

"Can we talk about it in the morning?"

"I just wanted you to know that I've . . . well, I've decided, my lovely boy. Do you want me to sing for you? Hush-a-by-baby?"

"Not now."

"You're so good, Bart. I just wanted to tell you that. Just wanted you to understand. Lovely boy. You're every-thing to me."

"Great."

"You're so . . ."

She hiccups. She turns, aims for the sofa, and hits the mark.

I'm not thinking about Ada anymore. Through half-open eyes, I look over at Mom, who has already started the motor saw in her mouth. Sometimes I wonder what it must be like to have your own room. I'd have pictures of Muhammad Ali and Bryn Terfel on the wall. A desk and a reading lamp over the bed. And a key to lock the door wouldn't be a bad thing.

In the morning, I only just manage to keep my eyes open when the alarm goes off. Mom is fast asleep with her mouth open and her clothes on.

We've got bread, jam, cheese, and milk. My lunch box is so full that I can hardly get the lid on.

Out in the hall, I find one of my posters on the floor. All crumpled up. I go back into the apartment and get more tape. Then I flatten the paper against my thigh and hang it up again. At the bottom I write: *Please leave this up*.

I'm met at the school gates by Ada.

"Come with me!"

She doesn't ask, she orders. I follow her down the corridor and into the basement. This is where the changing rooms, woodwork room, and music room are. She opens the door to one of the bathrooms at the end of the corridor and pulls me in. My back knocks into the sink. She locks the door behind us. I breathe in Ada through my nostrils and am sure that she's honey melon today. She didn't smell like that yesterday. We're standing far too close. I hold my breath and try to keep claustrophobia at bay. What's going on now?

"Sing for me," she says.

"I can't sing in here."

"I want to hear what it sounds like."

"Why?"

"Just try singing."

I should have hoofed it straight back out. Left her with some comment about not wanting to stand there and make a fool of myself. But it's Ada who's asking. She's not doing it to laugh at me. At least, I don't think she is.

I close my eyes. Try to think I'm in the bathroom at home. Picture the shower curtain, the cabinet with all the pills in it, and the mirror that's too high opposite me. There's a catastrophic drought going on in my mouth and my throat is performing some weird kind of self-strangulation act. I tense my stomach muscles, take a deep breath, and sing to burst an eardrum. It's hideous. Just as awful as it will sound if I go out onto the stage for the summer show.

I'm about to stop when Ada takes my hand. Slips her fingers through mine. She has a warm hand. I don't open my eyes. Instead I keep singing and suddenly something happens that's impossible to explain. Suddenly my voice returns from the spiky wilds and the notes are pure as water from a glacier. The more I sing, the better it sounds.

I'm singing for Ada. In a dirty school bathroom. And it sounds good. Not fantastic, but definitely good enough to be part of the summer show.

I stop abruptly and open my eyes.

"You sing really well."

"That's not the point."

"It's not?"

"I mean . . . well, yes."

We look down at our entwined hands. I let go as if I've had an electric shock.

"I don't know what happened," I say.

"I think you can do it."

We're standing very close. Too close. It's like I suddenly have problems breathing. I knock my back on the sink again.

"Sorry, but we can't really hold hands onstage."

I open the bathroom door and walk back toward the stairs.

"Wait, Bart. There's something I wanted to tell you."

"I just need . . ."

There's air and space and people on the playground. I stand at the edge and breathe deeply. So it really is possible. Not only was another living person there when I sang in tune, but she was standing right next to me. Are magic hands what are needed, or can I do it without holding on to someone? Before I can think any further, August comes over.

"What's up?"

I give a brief nod. Does he know that I've been in the bathroom with Ada?

"Is it true what they're saying, or what?"

"What's that?" I ask, and don't have a clue what he's talking about.

A couple of the other boys are standing at a distance watching. August raises his eyebrows. Whatever it is, it's coming now.

"That you live in a slum and your mom weighs three hundred pounds."

My body feels like it's been filled with cement.

"No," I say in a hard voice. "It's not true."

"What does she weigh, then?"

"Around one thirty."

And as I say it, I'm pretty sure that it's true. It's the only way I can make it sound convincing.

"Oh, right."

No one knows how much their mom weighs.

Especially not if it's a skinny wisp of a mother weighing 130 pounds. So August just nods. Part of me hopes that's it. That he realizes that Ada is spreading vicious lies and that this never needs to go any further. That Ada's told August in a moment of weakness. That it's all a stupid misunderstanding. That the boys over there haven't overhead anything. That I might be able to hire a tall thin lady who can say that she's my mom, and that we live in a normal building where people clean the stairs once a week.

Another part of me knows that this is just the beginning.

"Hmm, I think I can smell mold," August says, and walks off.

Almost right after, Marita comes over with a worried expression on her face and wonders if it's as bad as they say.

"I don't think so," I say.

"Do you live in . . . public housing?"

"If a four-bedroom apartment with a balcony and three fireplaces is called public housing, then yes, I guess I do," I reply.

"Three fireplaces?"

"Well, one's a wood-burning stove."

A couple of other people come over to ask the same thing before we're herded into the classroom. I can't see Ada anywhere. Where is she? The class starts and Ada's place remains empty. Maybe she's scared? No one wants someone who collects mass murderers as an enemy. And now there's absolutely no doubt: Ada can't keep a secret.

My mind is flooded with a massive amount of thoughts. I actually want Mom to come with all her pounds to the summer show and everything else at school. I don't need to live in a four-bedroom apartment with two fireplaces and a wood-burning stove. But you walk the line every day. A few more pushes and then Bertram and I will swap places. The only thing that can outweigh the fact that I live in a slum and my mom is a sumo wrestler is if I can sing so that people's jaws drop at the summer show.

The teacher tells us that the last hour of the day will be used for rehearsing. Anyone who wants to can use the auditorium during the breaks as well.

I really do try to follow the lesson. It's about the Norwegian language. A language that I speak and should know more about. But I don't learn anything today. When the bell rings, I stay sitting where I am until the teacher asks me to go out for some fresh air.

"I'm looking forward to hearing you sing later," he says as I pass him.

Out on the playground, it's not all about me. The others are talking about another sensation. Apparently Bertram was rapping in the auditorium and apparently he's as good as Snoop Dogg. His artist name is Femmer'n, a kind of Norwegian version of 50 Cent.

I look around. Bertram is not hovering on the edge of the playground. He's standing right by us. Like he's on his way in and someone else has to go out.

There's also a rumor that Class B have choreographed a dance that will give the audience a heart attack.

Not long ago, I saw a movie about the French Revolution on TV. It was almost as if I knew what it felt like to have your head under the guillotine. A great big sharp blade that was coming for your neck and soon your head would be hanging on a pole at the edge of the playground.

It gets harder and harder to follow the classes as the day goes by. It's like I'm not wired the right way. *Everything will be all right,* I normally tell myself. What kind of bullshit is that?

Not.

* * *

I stand on the stage. It's real. Even if it is just the splintered old stage in the school auditorium. It's the last class of the day and we're supposed to be rehearsing for the summer concert and I know that I should be anywhere other than here. And yet here I am, standing in the middle of the stage, swallowing air.

The teacher smiles at me and asks something I can't make out. Ada has not shown up yet. The others are staring at me in anticipation. It doesn't matter that my mom's as big as a barrel and I live in a building that's falling down, if only my singing is fantastic.

"I suggest you sing the same piece as on the recording."

"What?"

"It's Mozart."

"How do you know?"

"Because I like classical music. I've downloaded it."

"I need to warm up my voice first."

"Oh yes, I suppose you do."

"I'll just go down to the changing room to do it."

"Okay, we'll run through something else in the meantime."

I go down to the changing room, then down the hall and into the office. There I ask the lady for an address and she gives it to me on a yellow Post-it note. Then I rush as fast as I can out the door that's farthest away from the auditorium and don't look back.

I've never thought about it before, but the neighborhood around the school is very varied. There are old buildings and new buildings and an elegant area with big and small houses. I've heard people say that people with and without much money live here. There aren't many areas like this left in town. And when I stand in front of Ada's house, I can see that there really are differences.

I have to double-check the number and read the name on the mailbox. Ada doesn't live in a palace, but it wouldn't surprise me if a butler in uniform opened the door.

The woman who does open the door is more like a suitably weary mother with expensive jewelry.

"Is Ada in?" I ask.

"She is. I don't think I've seen you around here before."

"I haven't been here before. We're in the same class."

"And you are . . . called . . ."

"Bart."

"Ah yes, I've heard about you. Ada had supper with you."

Has Ada told absolutely everyone about me and Mom?

"Could I speak to her?"

"Just go along to her room. Fourth door on the left down the hall."

Fourth door on the left? We have one door into the apartment and one to the bathroom.

I take off my shoes and walk past a big living room, an enormous bathroom, and a closed door before I find myself standing in front of the fourth door. I lift my hand to knock on it, but it stops midway between my body and the door. Am I angry and disappointed? Should I act as if nothing's happened? Yell at her and then leave? Turn into the crazy mass murderer she thinks I am? I've got no plan. My feelings are at war and no one is winning.

I guess it's not possible to change. I'm generally positive about life. No one is evil. The world is a cool place. Or can I change everything?

Before I have time to knock, Ada is suddenly standing in the doorway. Not because she has telepathic abilities, but more likely because she was on her way to the bathroom or to fry some quail eggs in the kitchen.

"Oh," is all she says, and she swallows, making a loud gulping noise.

"I just came by," I say. She doesn't answer, so I keep going. "Like you came to see me yesterday."

The air goes out of her like she's got a puncture.

"Shall we . . . ?" she says, and points to her room.

"Nice room," I say, and peer in. "Nice house . . ."

"You don't need . . ."

It's the day for unfinished sentences. The kind that are loaded without you having to say all the words. Some might say there's a trace of sarcasm hidden in what I say. Maybe there is. Right now I don't have the brain power to find out.

Ada sits down on the chair in front of her desk. I can't be bothered to even begin describing all the computer stuff, iPods, and other gear in her room. Put it this way: it's not been cheap to furnish Ada's room.

"Are you ill?" I ask.

"Not very."

I look out the window to stop myself from staring at all the stuff in her room. There's a trampoline and a badminton net in the backyard. But no swimming pool.

"Listen, Bart, I know . . . I mean, I didn't mean to tell Lise, but I'm not very good at keeping secrets. Lise wanted to know where I'd been and I didn't want to lie to her. She's my best friend, you see. And maybe she didn't realize that she wasn't supposed to tell anyone else. I think maybe I forgot to say. Suddenly she'd sent a text to Gabriel, who knows August really well. I understand if you're mad at me. I just . . . didn't think."

"I didn't ask for an explanation."

"But I wanted to explain, or at least try. You see, I don't think I like secrets. Does everyone at school know?"

I shrug. Then something strange happens. It's like there's an explosion somewhere at the top of my nose. Have I suddenly got a deadly disease?

I'm not the sort to feel sorry for myself. That just makes you sad. And does no one any good.

I turn away and stand with my back to her. Because I have an idea of what kind of explosion could come next.

I'll be honest, I haven't cried since I was really little. And if it's going to happen again, it must not under any circumstance happen with a girl who I don't know if I hate or like, but who I certainly don't trust.

"Are you all right?" Ada asks.

If she had put a hand on my shoulder, I'm not sure the dam would have held. But luckily she's at least three feet behind me and doesn't move. The pressure at the top of my nose subsides. I manage to turn around again and say: "Yes, of course, I'm fine."

"I'm really sorry, Bart."

"It's okay. And you don't need to keep saying my name."

"Okay, but I really am sorry."

"Is that why you went home from school?"

Now it's her turn to nod and stare at the floor.

"Did you tell your mom as well?"

She snaps back her head.

"No, I've just told her nice things about you. Not that I'd have anything horrible to say about your mom to anyone, but—"

"Okay," I interrupt.

Then we stand there in her far-too-big room and hear all the sounds from far away. It doesn't make the atmosphere any better, but I don't think it makes it any worse.

"Do you want to hear some of the music I like?" Ada asks.

"Maybe."

She doesn't have the world's worst taste in music. I think possibly I do. I'd guessed it might be R&B or rap or hits that everyone likes, but she plays girls with acoustic guitars. The sort that sound kind of grown-up and are suited to dark autumn evenings and candlelight. In a way they suit Ada too. It's just the house that's wrong. A bit like we've snuck into the royal palace.

I stay for supper. They don't serve Russian caviar and sushi. We have tacos, and Ada's mom makes a real mess.

"Where do you live?" she asks with her mouth full of food.

"In an apartment," I say.

"Apartments are nice."

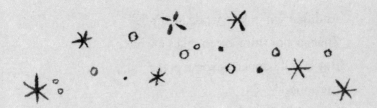

My seventh chapter

My posters are still hanging up on the wall when I get home. Mom is sitting at the table and has obviously just eaten. The bread, the jam, the cheese, the leftovers from yesterday—all that's left is the packaging.

"Hello, lovely boy. Will you help me tidy up?" she says.

I find a bag in the cupboard and throw the trash away.

"Mom, are we really going to move?"

She looks out the window, as if she's studying something in the far distance. I don't normally ask questions like that. It never does any good. I can't explain why I did just now, but I've got no intention of taking it back.

"Of course we're going to move, Bart. But we have to find the right place first."

"And that will take a while, won't it?"

"That sort of thing often takes a while."

"But it will happen at some point?"

"I promise."

"Good. That's all I wanted to know."

"Could you go down to McDonald's and get supper?"

She gives me some money and I put on my sneakers. Out in the hallway there's a man reading my flyer. His hair is wiry and he's got a few whiskers on his chin. He notices me and stabs at the poster with his finger.

"You seen this?" he asks.

"Eh, yes, sort of."

"Damn good idea. S'just what's needed. Someone with guts to sort out this dump."

"It was, well . . . it was actually me who put up the poster."

"You're joking? S'good. I'll be there."

"Great."

"When?"

"Sunday."

"What day's it today?"

"Friday."

"Two days. S'good. Got no board meetings on Sunday. Finish work early."

"Okay."

"Just kidding. Don't work, y'see. But I'll be there. I mean it. Cool dude, that's you."

I feel my cheeks flush. I'm not so sure he's a world champion at tidying up, but that doesn't really matter. He liked my poster and says he'll come. What if there are more like him?

I go to the supermarket instead of McDonald's, and buy more bread and things to put on it. When I get home, Mom's fallen asleep in front of the TV. After I've had something to eat, I turn off the TV and go into the bathroom to sing. The pills in the medicine cabinet vibrate. The sink tap is dripping more than usual. Then I try to imagine Ada standing beside me holding my hand. And again, I manage to keep more or less on track.

I've never been to the opera. I once saw a man singing opera in the street, but Mom dragged me away. So I can hardly say that I've experienced any opera. But you don't need to have seen fat ladies and men in weird costumes to know that you like it. I found something on YouTube, but it was just some guy with crooked teeth from an *Idol*-type program in England. I haven't learned the difference between Mozart or Beethoven or Wagner or Puccini. There's a whole load of other composers too, but most of them were dead before even my grandmother was born.

I look at the top of my head in the mirror. I only need a few more inches. I don't want to be a giant.

When I come out of the bathroom, Mom's woken up.

"Can you get me the remote control?"

"Here you go," I say, and put it in her hand.

As Mom turns on the TV, the doorbell rings. My first thought is that it's Ada standing outside. Mom makes some head movements to indicate that I should go and find out. The face I see through the peephole is wrinkly and familiar. I tiptoe back to Mom on the sofa and whisper: "It's Grandma."

Mom looks at me in horror.

"She wasn't supposed to come today. I told her I was working Friday and Saturday evening. Don't let her in."

"But it's Grandma, Mom."

There's another ring on the bell. I notice beads of sweat on Mom's forehead. With Mom, stress often comes out as sweat.

"Get me a blanket. I'll pretend I'm sick," she says.

I give her a woolen blanket and then open the door.

"There you are, and you're both here," Grandma says. "You certainly took your time opening the door, given how big the apartment is."

"I had to help Mom first. She's not well," I explain.

Grandma comes in with a suitably big plastic bag.

"I was in the neighborhood, so I thought I'd come by with this," she says, and puts the bag down. The contents are well packed. "Are you having a big birthday party this weekend?"

Grandma doesn't mean to be spiteful with her questions, but they're often hard to answer. I always have to think twice before saying anything to her. Mom and I have mostly agreed what we're going to say beforehand, but sometimes I get a bit confused about what we've told her.

"I'm going to have a birthday party with my friends next week," I lie. "But I hope that you can come on Sunday."

"Of course I'll come."

"But I have to tell you that there's going to be a big cleanup here on Sunday."

"Yes, I saw the poster, Bart. I'd be more than happy to help."

"Oh, that's great."

Grandma turns to Mom and asks one of her awkward questions. "Funny, isn't it, that you work in Telenor, but your phone doesn't work?"

"Oh, there's been some trouble with the . . . network," Mom says.

"Better that it happens to the staff than the customers," I add.

"Yes, I guess it is," Grandma agrees with one of her strange looks.

In the cupboard over the stove, there's a magic box. Mom puts all the bills in it. And once they're in, they rarely come out again. It's almost like they get sucked into a black hole. But only almost. A blocked cell phone proves in a way that the bills still exist.

Grandma does the dishes and tidies up a bit. Like she always does. She never asks what's wrong with Mom. Instead, she makes coffee and asks if I need help with anything.

Grandma is pretty much everything that Mom isn't. That doesn't mean that everything Grandma does is perfect. She smokes those cigarettes you roll yourself, and according to Mom, she's had more boyfriends than most people have pants. I think she's done with men now, because she lives on her own with a chatty parrot called Gudleik. She talks to him like they were married. We never go to visit her because Mom says she's allergic to birds, but I'm not sure that's true.

"Got any further with moving?" Grandma asks.

"Within a month or so," Mom replies.

I want to say it's not true. That Mom's lying and that we won't be moving in the near future. I don't know if Grandma believes anything we say anymore, but she seems happy enough with Mom's answer.

"Oh, won't it be nice," she says with that strange look on her face again.

On Sunday it's my birthday. I'm going to be a teenager. And I'm sure I'll see the world in a whole new way.

"I've been thinking about the boxing," Mom says when Grandma's left and it's almost time for bed. "Perhaps it's not the right thing for you after all?"

Mom has turned off the sound on the TV. She only does that when we're going to have a serious talk. Maybe the coach has called her.

"Why's that?"

"Well, there's another sport that's made up of all the skills you need to survive. Mixed martial arts. It's like boxing, wrestling, and kickboxing all rolled into one.

You learn to throw, punch, and kick, and evidently it was an Olympic sport in the old days."

"I dunno."

"Think about it, you'd be able to defend yourself no matter what your attacker does."

"I might not be attacked that much."

"They teach you to have no fear. I saw something about it on a morning show."

"Is it okay if I do some research first?" I ask as I get out the computer and log on to the neighbor's network.

Some swift googling reveals that it's a sport that allows almost everything except biting and poking someone in the eye. Luckily, competitions and fights are banned in Norway and it's hardly going to be taught to boys my age.

"It says here there's a movie about it called *Fight Club*. Maybe we should watch that first?" I suggest.

"Yes. Oh, that reminds me, I borrowed a movie about boxing that I thought we could watch this evening. Look."

She holds up a cover of a boy leaping in the air. The movie's called *Billy Elliot*.

"Have you read the back?" I ask, skimming the text.

"No, but Cheap Charlie said that it was about someone who did boxing."

"It sounds like he would rather do ballet."

"Really? Ballet?"

She snatches the movie from me and reads the back. Mom always tries her best, but it doesn't always turn out the way she thinks. A movie about a boy who does boxing but would rather do ballet might well be good. But it's hardly going to make me any keener on boxing.

"Hmm, that's not right, then. I'll go down and ask him if he's got anything else."

She's soon back with a movie called *The Fighter*. She's been told that it is definitely about a boxer who doesn't want to do anything else.

It's not Mom's evening. The boxer in the movie doesn't want to do anything else, but it's mainly about his brother, who's as high as most of the people in our building. And there's a mom in the movie too, and she's nothing like my mom, but a bit similar all the same. It's so hard to explain things like that. Mom doesn't really like the movie, and that means that I don't really enjoy it either. And in any case, people getting beaten up is not really what I need today. It doesn't feel like the movie's going to have a happy ending, but you never know.

We eventually switch to a prime-time talk show on television before the movie is finished.

"Sorry," Mom says.

"It was good," I reassure her.

The good thing about Saturdays is that there's no school. And the good thing about days off is that you can do whatever you like.

The only thing I don't have is something sensible to do.

Mom gets up before me. She mixes some muesli with water and lots of jam and sugar for breakfast.

"I was thinking about working two days in the supermarket this week," she tells me.

"Very good," I say.

"And I've been thinking about your tidying-up project."

I look up from my cereal.

"Yes, and I thought I could maybe be a kind of project manager."

"Of course you can."

"You do know that it's . . . well, highly likely that no one will come?"

"I met someone on the stairs who said he would come."

"Yes, but some of them talk nonsense."

"I trust him," I say, and look down at my cereal.

Mom sits down on the sofa after breakfast and turns

on the TV. I go into the bathroom to sing. Halfway through the song I half open my eyes and catch half my face in the mirror. Every time I meet my own eyes, my voice rasps off-key. As soon as I close my eyes again, I'm back in tune. I've read about hypnotism on the Internet. Maybe I could trick myself into believing that I'm standing in our bathroom when I'm actually performing in front of hundreds of people?

I go out and plop down next to Mom. It's a repeat of *Charter Fever*. I've never taken a vacation to another country, but if the people in the program are anything to go by, it looks a bit wild. But I do think I'd like staying in a hotel. It looks clean.

After a couple of hours in front of the TV, I say to Mom: "I think I'll go out for a bit."

"Where are you going?"

"Just for a walk."

"Well, don't go too far, then."

"I won't."

Sometimes Mom and I step on each other's toes on weekends. So it's good to get away for a few hours.

At school, they're always talking about how important it is to use your body. Maybe I should suggest it to Mom, but it might seem like I was making fun of her.

My posters are still hanging there. At the bottom of one, where I've written *Please leave this up*, someone has added in very wobbly letters: *dammit come*.

I laugh to myself and go out. As the door closes behind me, I see three familiar faces in front of me. I stop abruptly. Some of the people I meet five times a week, but never on a Saturday and never here, are standing out back. Of all the people I don't want to meet in the backyard, I think these three rank highest.

"What are you doing here?" just pops out of my mouth.

An invisible hand is squeezing my stomach. Because August, Gabriel, and Johnny are standing there. Three boys from my class. Three boys who never just happen to be in my neighborhood. I could have saved myself the question, since I already know the answer.

"We wanted to see if it was true," August says. "Is this your slum?"

What do you answer to that? *No, this is someone else's slum.*

"Is that your dad?" Gabriel asks, pointing to some drunken bum who's struggling to open the door.

I could of course say, *No, he's not my dad.* But getting an answer is not the point. They want to laugh at me. In exactly the same way that they've laughed at Bertram for years. Bertram, who's now called Femmer'n and is going to rap at the end-of-year concert, Bertram who's emerging from the darkest recesses of the playground.

"Can we see your mom?" August asks.

I really have nothing to say. There's no way out of this. I don't know that I even want to explain anything at all. But the worst thing is August asking about Mom. As though she were some freak at a sideshow.

August is the biggest kid in the class and the arm-wrestling champion. I do boxing and the coach has said that it's about time that I started to pack a punch.

He's right. I know he is.

The trio have closed in on me. August is smiling. For a brief moment it almost looks like a nice smile.

But it's not.

My balled fist flies through the air. On its way toward August's cheek. The strength, the curve, the direction, everything's perfect. A punch that Muhammad Ali would have been proud of.

But my fist carries on past August's face, as though I'm dancing, not boxing.

Just when I manage to stop the movement, it hits. It feels like something exploding in my face. My head is thrown back and I feel my legs buckle. I can't see August and the others anymore. I can see the sky. A lot of sky. And a bit of roof.

August, Gabriel, and Johnny bend down over me. They say something to each other. Someone has put a whistle in my ears. I can't read their lips.

The boys disappear from my sky. Something runs down my cheek. It's not raining.

I didn't just stand there and take it. I hit back. It's maybe hard to believe, but I'm actually quite proud of myself.

"Whoa, are you okay?"

Another face leans in across the sky.

"What did those assholes do that for anyway?"

The guy who read my poster and said he was coming on Sunday helps me sit up. I gingerly touch my face. My fingers turn red. The guy takes off his T-shirt and pushes it into my face.

"Ow," I cry.

"Sorry, kid. Think you'll need something done with your nose."

"My nose?"

"Think it's broken."

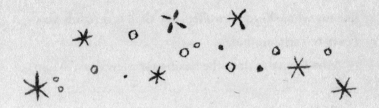

My eighth chapter

It could have been worse. I could have smashed my head on the ground and gone out like a shooting star. Mom would have been left on her own. She couldn't have coped with that.

"How unlucky to fall and hit your face against the banister," Mom says, and rubs my back.

The guy with the T-shirt just nodded when I told her about my incredibly unlucky fall. Before we went to the hospital, he whispered in my ear: "Next time I'll help you get the bastards."

I'm sitting in front of the TV now with a nose that has been snapped back into place and bandaged to keep it in the right position. Both my eyes are purple. It feels like my whole head is swollen. My skull is certainly very heavy to carry around.

"You'll have to drop the boxing for a few days," Mom says.

"Yeah, maybe."

"Should I take down your notices about the cleanup on Sunday?"

"No, it's only my nose. I haven't broken my arm or leg."

Mom smiles at me.

"You're always so positive, my lovely boy. Is it all right if I go out for a little while this evening?"

"This evening?"

"I'll be back early. I promise. I'll just go out for a quick one, guaranteed. But if you'd rather I stayed at home, I will. I'll only go if you're okay with it."

I look at Mom. She tilts her head and smiles at me. I really don't want her to go.

"Yes, it's fine."

"Good, Bart, thank you. I won't be gone long at all. Just need to get some air. It can get so stuffy in here sometimes."

She shakes her large body.

"I know."

It's like there's someone jumping on my face the

102

whole time. Mom gives me two aspirin, but that doesn't stop the elephants stomping across my face. It's hard to follow even the dumbest programs on TV. Hope they've not killed off my brain at the same time.

Mom puts on some makeup and goes out. I turn the TV off. It hurts more to lie down than sit up.

On Monday it'll be official. I'll have to pull out of the summer show. I never intended to sing anyway. I'll explain that my sinuses are swollen along with the rest of my face and that it means that I sing so out of tune that people's ears will bleed. And then I can give August a dirty look so that everyone knows that he's the one to blame.

I test my voice. A fine, pure note rolls out. Nothing shatters. No ears will suffer a terrible death. But I can't bear to sing for too long. My head weighs a ton.

I turn the TV on again and try to watch a comedy series where the canned laughs explode at things I don't understand. And the news is full of tragedies.

Just as I'm dozing off, the doorbell rings. I look through the peephole and see the face of the guy who helped me.

"How's it going?" he asks when I open the door.

"Bit sore," I reply, and wait before saying: "Do you want to come in?"

"Is your mom at home?"

"No."

Then there he is in the middle of the room, looking around. The guy's basically skin and bone and a couple of teeth that a dentist should look at.

"My name's Bart," I say without holding out my hand.

"Go there quite a lot."

"What?"

"The bar."

"Oh right. What's your name?"

"Geir."

"Oh, I think there was someone here looking for you the other day."

"That's me. I just vanish. Poof, gone and no one can find me. Mostly when I owe money."

"I said you were dead."

"Hehe, cool. Rumors of my death are definitely exaggerated."

Geir plops down on the sofa and shifts position a couple of times. He rubs his hands up and down his thighs. I go over and sit on my bed.

"Why'd he thump you, then?" Geir asks.

"I hit him first. Or, well . . . I tried to hit him first. I go to boxing, but I haven't really started punching yet."

"Boxing's dead cool. Watching it, at least. When they're good. You were floored pretty quick. You haven't learned any guards yet?"

"Yes, but I didn't have time."

"See this." He points to a scar by his eye. "I was too slow too. You don't speed on heroin, hehe."

"What happened?"

"Broke my jaw and stuff. Was in the hospital for weeks. But the drugs were free drugs, so that's cool."

"I mean, who did it?"

"I owed money. Gets you into trouble quick. I often owe money."

I start to get nervous that Mom might come home. She's always saying that I shouldn't talk to the other tenants. Like I might become a hardened addict if I just speak to them. It's all happened rather fast, but I've already decided: Geir is my friend. Perhaps not someone I trust one hundred percent, but someone who can drop by as long as he doesn't steal anything.

Geir starts to tell me about when he was young. When he was an ordinary boy with ordinary dreams, who didn't think he would do anything wrong in his life. I guess that's what they mean when they say *going off the rails*. For a while it sounds like he blames everything and everyone else: bad friends, bad luck, parents, too-strong drugs, and a horrible girlfriend.

"But you know," he says after a while, "only one who's to blame, really, for me being here now is me. I'll show you something."

He pulls up one of his pant legs and reveals a skinny leg full of revolting sores. I try not to look too hard.

"Not doing this so you'll think I'm disgusting. I only want to scare you. I've done this to myself. You'd think I was screwed up. Sad thing is that I'm not. All my screws are in place."

He rolls his pant leg back down.

"Can't you stop?"

"I'm sure I could, Bart. But I don't succeed."

Geir is a nice man who makes me depressed. Whenever something good happened in his life, a kind of monster shadow fell over it all. It's easier when we talk about everyday things that aren't about life on the edge and sores that are painful. Suddenly he stands up and says that he has to go.

"I've got an important meeting and stuff. But I'll be there tomorrow," he promises.

"Are you normally punctual?"

"No, but tomorrow I will be."

When he's gone, I take a couple of aspirin and go to bed. Mom was going to come home early, but it's not early anymore.

Some mornings are far too quiet. As though one of the most important sounds in the world is missing. I look over at the sofa. Where Mom should be lying and snoring. The sofa is empty.

The clock says it's seven thirty. Mom has come home early the next day a few times before. And every time she's promised that it will never happen again.

I lie in bed and gingerly touch my nose and the surrounding area. It feels like the whole front of my face has come loose.

I know that I should be lying here thinking: *Yes, today is my birthday.* I'm officially a teenager now. But my head is full of a mix of Mom, Ada, Geir, pain, and boys at school with hard fists.

Yippee . . .

As nothing happens in the next ten minutes, I get up. There's a cake recipe lying on the counter. But it doesn't look like we've got any of the ingredients. I pour some water over my cereal and empty what's left of the sugar over it.

If a birthday starts badly, it can only get better. Most birthdays should get better as the day goes on. It would be a lot worse if a birthday ended badly.

I know where Grandma's present is, but don't want to open it without her. So instead I start to sing. It's hard to judge how well you sing yourself, but isn't that better than normal? As if my broken nose has cleaned out my sinuses and the last out-of-tune notes from my voice.

I sing so loudly that people start to bang on the floor and walls. My invisible audience is perfect. I finish by singing happy birthday to me at the top of my voice.

Then I log on to the Internet and look for photographs of John Jones. This time I discover a photo that I've not seen before. A man in uniform, sitting on a chair, leaning forward with his elbows on his thighs. But there's something that's not right. I enlarge the picture. He's got false legs. Those metal things with two shoes on. Maybe I'm getting a bit desperate now, but does he not look a bit like me? Something about the snub nose, hair color, and the thick eyebrows?

What if that was Dad? He's in a book of portraits of American soldiers who lost body parts in Iraq. I click on a woman with no right arm, a man who is missing one eye, and a soldier with burn scars all over his body. The publisher's e-mail address is at the bottom of the Web page, so I write an e-mail:

Dear Sir or Madam,

My name is Bart, and I live in Norway. It is at the top of Europe.

My dad's name is John Jones. I think you have a picture of him in your book. He disappeared before I was born. I think he just liked my mother for a very short time.

Can you give him this e-mail? And tell him that it is not important how many legs he has. He is a hero to me. I will be more than happy if he gets in touch.

Yours truly,

Bart Narum

P.S. It is my birthday today.

I found a good online dictionary. Before I have time to decide whether it's a good idea or not, I've pressed *send*. If I don't take any chances, I'll never find him. The mail is on its way now.

We have a rule at school that for your party you invite either the whole class or all your classmates of the same sex. So I've actually been invited to loads of birthday parties. No one has asked me not to come. But I never tell Mom about the invitations. Because then she would no doubt run out and buy nice clothes and presents that we can't afford. Have to say, I think it sounds pretty exhausting to be in the limelight for a whole evening. And if you don't have a party, you don't need to invite anyone. I'm looking forward to opening Grandma's present, though; she's good at presents. Better than Mom, who doesn't always manage to buy something in time. She tells me that I'll get an extra-special Christmas present instead.

I look at the clock again. It's nearly one. Where is Mom? She's never been this late before.

I turn on the TV and stare at it without really watching the program. I check the time at regular intervals. It's a gray birthday outside. I put on my shoes and go out. Mom doesn't usually tell me which bar she's going to, but I know that she often goes to Wild Beers and it's only a couple of blocks away. When I get there, it's closed and doesn't open again until four.

Someone's fighting on the TV when I get home. There's loud music coming from the apartment next door. I sit on the sofa and wait. My birthday is just about to get better. I'm sure it's just about to happen. It's raining outside now.

No one is fighting on TV anymore, but there are people fighting out on the stairs. It looks like it's going to stop raining. At two o'clock I get a glass of water and take two more aspirin.

Suddenly the doorbell rings. I see Grandma through the peephole and finally I feel a nice feeling flooding through me.

"Hi, Grandma," I say happily as I open the door.

I expect a hug and happy birthday. But she looks at me with an odd expression. As though she's hurting somewhere. Is there something wrong with Grandma?

"Something's happened, Bart."

"Where does it hurt?"

"Not to me."

I know immediately who she's talking about.

"No!"

"It's not as serious as it sounds," Grandma continues.

She's still standing out in the hallway. That means it has to be serious.

"Your mom's been admitted to the hospital," she tells me.

Of course I should have realized that. Mom's sick

again. Now I should break down and sob inconsolably. But I say nothing. Just look at Grandma as if I don't know what a hospital is.

"Can I come in?"

I'm obviously standing in the way, and I move to one side so she can come in.

"Your mom was at the bar last night and I think she drank rather a lot. As she does sometimes," Grandma explains.

"Not that often. And less now than before."

"Yes, I'm sure, but yesterday she had a bit too much. And she collapsed. Well, you know, what with the diabetes and the heart murmur. She's not in very good shape, but they'll sort it all out at the hospital."

"We have to go and visit her."

"We will. But she's not awake at the moment."

"Is she asleep?"

"No, she's . . . well, she's in a kind of coma."

"Coma? Like, she won't wake up even when there's a lot of noise?

"She will wake up, but it might just take some time. She . . . well . . . I don't know . . ."

Grandma sits down on the sofa. The sofa where Mom should have been snoring last night. I position myself where Mom normally has her head. Grandma is looking at me all the time. I don't know if she's checking to see if I've got feelings, and will react instantly if I totally lose it. Grandma stretches out her hand so her fingertips touch my shoulder.

"We can't cancel the cleanup," I say.

"Do you really think you can face it?"

"I know I can face it."

I've seen people talking to patients in a coma on TV and then they suddenly wake up and everyone cries. I think it was probably some stupid series.

"What happened to you?" Grandma asks.

I'd almost forgotten about my nose.

"Oh, I had a fight with someone in my class."

Grandma shuffles up the sofa and puts her arm around me.

"I'm sorry that your life seems to be so hard."

"Broken noses mend."

"They do."

"It'll be as good as new. That's what the doctor said."

"Good."

It just sounds fake and empty when I'm positive. I can hear it myself. And she's sitting so close that I can smell the cigarette smoke and hear the wheeze in her throat. Grandma could die any moment. She doesn't deserve this.

"Grandma," I say, and look her straight in the eye. "Do you believe what Mom and I tell you?"

I think she attempts a smile. But smiles that aren't heartfelt often end up as grimaces.

"Your mother does the best she can. I'm absolutely certain of that. And she so wishes everything was better than it is. But yes, I know that she doesn't always tell the truth."

"She doesn't work for Telenor."

"I know."

"She lies all the time. And I do too. We agree beforehand what we're going to say to you, what our lies are."

"I know that you lie, Bart."

"Is that why you get such a funny face sometimes?"

"Do I?"

"Why haven't you said anything?"

"Would it make things any better?"

"I'm sorry . . . for telling lies."

She strokes my arm. Her technique is different from Mom's. I miss Mom's big, soft hands.

"Oh sweetie, sorry. I forgot to say happy birthday," she whispers in my ear. "Happy birthday, Bart."

"Thank you."

And we sit like this for a while. Grandma cries without making a sound. I look out the window and wonder how to organize the cleanup. Of course I should be thinking about Mom, but I'm sure there will be plenty of time to think about her later.

"Can you be the project manager for the cleanup?" I ask.

Grandma lets go of me and dries her tears.

"The cleanup?"

"Yes, we need someone who's done it before and knows what needs to be done."

"Yes, well, some tidying up and . . . yes, perhaps it's mostly tidying up."

"I think we should clean a bit as well."

"Cleaning is a good idea. Uff, of course, I've got a present for you as well."

"I know where it is."

I find it in a pile of clothes and give it to Grandma, who then gives it back to me with another *happy birthday*.

Grandma doesn't have much money. If she did, she would no doubt give more to Mom. But the present is so much more than I expected. And I'm sure she bought it the honest way.

"Thank you," I say, my voice a bit wobbly.

The picture on the box is unmistakable. It's a smartphone.

"I'll pay for your contract. That way it'll be possible to get hold of at least one of you. Do you think it's all right?"

"It's . . . it's more than all right."

It's all a bit much at once, really. It's at times like this I wish I had my own room. But all we've got is the bathroom, and that's not the same.

I've got a cell phone. A good cell phone.

I give Grandma a hug and hold on. I feel that pressure at the base of my nose, my eyes aren't clear, and I don't make a sound. I don't know how long we sit like that, but I wouldn't be surprised if it was longer than the usual grandma hug.

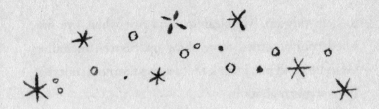

My ninth chapter

"Sorry, kid, tried to get as many here as I could. People do all kinds of weird things on a Sunday, you know. You wouldn't believe . . . shit, it wasn't easy."

Geir looks at me uncertainly. I should say something soon.

"It's . . . ," I start. "It's . . ."

"I know. Sorry."

I look from one person to the other. Like I'm worried that something has happened to my eyes. Maybe I'm seeing double after the punch on my nose.

"That's . . . great," I say.

"Oh, maybe it is. D'you mean it?"

I count twelve people. Twelve people who've come

to help tidy up. My cleanup. And just when I've finished counting, two more show up. Sixteen including Grandma and me. I think that's a good turnout, not that I know much about it.

"And . . . it's your birthday and things, so we thought we'd get you this . . . Or I did, anyway. But it's from us all."

He gives me a present wrapped in newspaper.

"Sorry, kid, couldn't find the wrapping paper," he explains. "Go on, open it."

As I unwrap the present, they sing the most out-of-tune *happy birthday* ever. It's a bike lock. With a key.

"Thank you. That's so kind of you," I say, and can't bring myself to tell them that I don't have a bike.

"Thought it might come in handy, living here and all that," Geir explains. "People don't leave your stuff alone."

"It's really nice."

"Yeah, and then . . . well, it's outside."

"What's outside?"

"You're not just getting the lock."

We go out, and there's a bike standing there. It doesn't look brand-new, but almost.

"I filed off the bike frame number myself," Geir whispers. "But I bought the lock in a shop."

I don't know whether to shake his hand or give him a hug, so I don't do either. Someone has lost their bike. And I've gained a bike. Suddenly I realize that I'm standing there hugging the lock.

"You deserve it," Geir says. "No one else in the building has done anything about tidying the place up. Well, we'd better get started. Plenty to do."

"Um, yes. This is my grandma, Lillian. She's going to be the boss," I say, pointing at Grandma, who is standing in the doorway looking a bit nervous.

It doesn't take long before she's gotten over her nerves and is ordering everyone around. Some are sent down into the cellar, others up to the attic, and three people are given the stairs. We should really have a Dumpster, but we put all the trash in the cans instead. I'll call the city council from my new phone on Monday and ask if they can come and pick it up.

"People can be real pigs," Geir says, as he holds out a bucketful of whole and broken syringes for me to see.

Just to be clear, it's not only drug addicts who live here. There's a woman from Somalia helping us clean up, and two Kurdish boys, and a man who must be about the same age as Grandma who tells us he's lived here since he was twenty. Geir says that a few of them are also on methadone, which he explains is a kind of drug for people who want to get off heroin.

They say it's the thought that counts. One man washes and cleans a spot by the mailboxes over and over again. A woman in skintight jeans keeps asking where she should put all this shit, but she never has anything in her hands.

We're at it for over two hours. Someone has even found some paint in the cellar and gets rid of the graffiti by the mailboxes. It's still not the nicest building in town, but some of the helpers say that they *almost want to come home now.*

I thank everyone afterward and shake each person's hand before pushing my bike around the streets. I wish I could just hop on and pedal off, but I think I'll leave learning to ride for another day.

Do you see the world differently when you're a teenager? It feels pretty grown-up to have organized a cleanup and to shake everyone by the hand. But it's only snotty-nosed kids who can't ride a bike.

I feel like I'm split, but think I can live with it.

When I get home, Grandma has baked the chocolate cake that Mom was going to make. It tastes even better when Grandma makes it, because she buys all the right ingredients. After all the cleaning and my walk with my bike, I could probably have eaten the whole thing, but I have to save some space for dinner.

"How about coming to stay with me for a few days?" Grandma asks.

"Do you know how far it is to school?" I ask with my mouth full of cake. "And boxing."

"You're right. And you might want to go out with your friends after school . . ."

"I don't have any friends."

"You don't?"

"I want to be honest now. I want to tell you the truth about my life."

"Honesty is . . . well, not something I'm used to. But there's Gudleik, and he needs food and . . ."

"You could take your parrot with you, since Mom's not here."

"Yes, yes, I could do that."

It's not hard to see that Grandma's a bit worried about living here. She looks around at the piles of magazines, clothes, and a couple of boxes full of I don't remember what. Someone shouts something out on the stairs.

"Most of the people who live here are nice, at least

ninety percent," I say, and regret it immediately.

If as many as ten percent are dangerous, this isn't somewhere you'd want to stay. But it's true, after all. Once we left our shopping bags outside the door for two minutes, and when we went back out to get them, they'd been stolen. And Mom was once threatened by a guy out in the hall, and the police are called so often that one time I said there was an empty apartment they could use as an office.

"Ninety-nine percent," I said, rounding it up. A little white lie has to be allowed. "Ninety-nine and a half."

"It's fine, Bart. I can stay here for a few days. But if Mom is in the hospital any longer, we'll have to think about going to my place. Agreed?"

"Yes. You can have my bed, and I can sleep on the sofa."

"That's very kind of you."

After dinner, we go up to Grandma's place to get Gudleik. On the bus back, he says *Where are my panties?* over and over again. The passengers laugh.

"I've no idea where he got that from," Grandma says with unusually red cheeks.

Then Gudleik follows up with: *Do I look fat in this?*

* * *

I don't know how to describe the evening. I miss Mom, of course. Now that there's nothing else going on, I think about her all the time. I've got a thousand questions, but Grandma can't answer any of them. No one can answer most of them. That sort of question is really annoying.

I'm going to demand that the doctors make her better than before. And I'm going to tell Mom that she has to get her act together. Do I sound mean when I say things like that?

I sit on the sofa and watch TV, and Gudleik makes comments all the time. *She looks ugly in that dress.*

"Was it a strange birthday for you?" Grandma asks.

"Apart from Mom, it was quite . . ."

The word *good* stops halfway. How can a day be good when my mom has ended up in the hospital?

"Strange, yes," I say instead.

"There will be better birthdays, just wait and see," Grandma reassures me.

"I've just sent my first text message."

"Who to?"

"A girl in my class who doesn't know how to keep her mouth shut about anything."

I said I was going to be honest with Grandma. I

found Ada's number on the Internet, and the text that it took me ages to write says: *Got a cell phone for my birthday. Now you can warn me in advance. Bart.*

"Do you like her, then?"

"We live in two separate worlds. And it's a bit weird when the two worlds meet."

"Opposites attract, they say."

"We're just friends. Or, at least, I think we're friends. I guess I have to find out."

"How romantic, Bart."

Sometimes grandmothers can make you sick. Gudleik says he's looking for his panties again.

I go into the bathroom and sing. Even though Grandma is sitting right outside the door, it sounds just as good as it did this morning. When I come out, she claps and gives me a hug that hurts my nose.

"You've got a fantastic voice."

"Thank you."

"You're so . . ."

"That's enough."

My cell makes a kind of swallowing noise. Ada writes: *Cool. Qpsa? Wot about smr shw? #-)*

I guess that she's talking about the summer show. I haven't given it a thought all day. I haven't even thought about what's going to happen when August and his buddies tell people about this weekend.

Things have happened, I reply to Ada.

Wot? she asks seconds later.

It's as if Grandma reads my mind when she asks: "Do you want to stay at home tomorrow?"

No doubt I sound like a chicken, but I nod slowly.

"We can go up to the hospital," Grandma suggests.

There's no point in putting it off, but right now I think I need a break, preferably several years.

"Okay."

The next instant I have an idea. The kind that just pops up when you least expect it. I write to Ada: *Tell you later. But I will sing at show. :-)*

"I need to go to boxing tomorrow," I say to Grandma.

"With that nose?"

"It's important."

The stupid thing about ideas is that they can steal your sleep. And Grandma's snoring is different from Mom's. And Mom has made hollows in the sofa that don't fit my body.

Luckily Gudleik shuts up as soon as Grandma puts a blanket over the cage.

When Grandma wakes me up, I'm exhausted. . . . The breakfast table is groaning under all that's on it, and Gudleik says, *This is the best day of your life.*

Grandma has called the hospital and can tell me that Mom has regained consciousness, but is still very weak.

"We can take some flowers," I say.

"Yes."

"If we've got enough money."

"Of course we have."

Grandma is not that old. She had Mom when she was very young and still together with Granddad. I've never met him. People tell me he moved to Sweden because alcohol is cheaper there. Grandma gets a disability allowance because she's in so much pain and gets tired so quickly. She worked in a Narvesen convenience store, selling cancer sticks, as she calls them. Even though she smokes herself.

I've visited Mom in the hospital before, but she's never been in a coma. It feels weird to be sitting on a tram in a wrinkled shirt and suit pants. When I come into her room, it smells clean and funny and Mom looks like she's asleep. She doesn't make a sound, and for a moment I think she's dead, but when I touch her arm, I can feel that it's warm. Grandma goes in search of a vase for the flowers. Mom doesn't wake up, even when Grandma drops the metal vase on the floor.

"We've got a meeting with the doctor," Grandma tells me.

He sits in a cramped office and says a lot of things that I don't think I understand. But I do understand some of it: Mom has to change her lifestyle. She has to eat better food and lose weight. Exercise more, or at least walk more. She has to get better at taking her medicine. But most important of all, she has to reduce what he calls her alcohol intake.

"So she shouldn't get drunk so often," I say.

"Preferably not at all," the doctor points out. "If she drinks, this could happen again. And it could be fatal."

"Fatal?"

"She might die."

The doctor looks at Grandma and asks: "Does he stay with you?"

"No, I'm staying with him."

"I mean normally. Is it you who looks after him?"

"No, he lives with his mother."

"I see."

The doctor jots something down in his papers. He asks if I have any questions, but suddenly I don't have any left. Certainly not that the doctor can answer.

Afterward, when we're sitting by Mom's bed, Grandma seems upset.

"She's just sleeping," I explain, as I'm not sure whether she thinks that Mom is still in a coma or not.

"I know. I just . . . I think he might contact Social Services."

"The doctor?"

"Yes."

We've had visits from Social Services before. Mom doesn't like them. But I think they're just doing their best. So I'm always extra happy when they come round. It must be a year or more since they were there last.

On the way home from the hospital, I get another text message from Ada: *Wassup? U @ home?*

I think she's asking if I'm at home.

I am sick. I look down at the text, decide to delete the *I am* and instead write: *Mom is sick.*

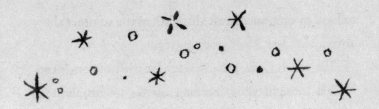

My tenth chapter

When I get to boxing, I go to speak to the coach first. He studies my nose from different angles.

"What happened?" he asks.

"I've starting fighting."

"Did you hit?"

I shake my head.

"Is it okay if I ask the others if they want to take part in a boxing demonstration at school?" I ask.

"A demonstration?"

"A pretend fight. It would be good advertising for the sport."

"I'm not sure that boxing needs advertising."

"But I need advertising. For me. Otherwise I'm going

to have to sing, and I can't sing. Not at the summer show, anyway."

The coach looks pensive. He's clearly not convinced.

"I'd thought about reading quotes by Muhammad Ali while the others demonstrate the noble art of boxing. And then give a bit of boxing history."

"Maybe it's not such a bad idea."

"And then I'll tell the school what I do. I thought that maybe some of the kids wouldn't bother me if they see the boxers I hang out with."

The coach looks at me closely.

"Does this have anything to do with your nose?"

"Maybe."

"Come on, let's ask the others."

The others don't say yes right away. Muhammad Ali and boxing history don't interest them as much as they do the coach. But when I tell them it's actually for me, Christian immediately says: "Of course we'll do it. No one's allowed to bother Bart."

It turns out that only Christian and Robert can do it, but two is actually perfect.

"That's great," I say.

I don't have to do any training today because of my nose. But I stay and watch the others. I read somewhere that you have to train for about 10,000 hours to be really good at a sport. I figure I've done about 40 hours of boxing so far. And I've only just started to punch. So that means I've got 9,960 hours left until I might perhaps fight in the Norwegian championship. And I've already got a broken nose, a black eye, and ringing in my ears.

I might perhaps want to use those 9,960 hours on something else. But I can't see myself in old-fashioned costumes with a big opera belly either. Maybe I'll do something that you don't need to spend 10,000 hours practicing to become good at. A mailman?

On the way home I sing. With no sound, but with my whole body and exaggerated mouth movements. I probably look like a lunatic, but I don't often meet people I know around here. The volume is up so high the sound is like wind in my ears. I stop on the bridge over the main road, look out over the town, and hold the note for a long, long time.

I'm exhausted when I get home, even though I haven't done any training or even used my voice. I lie in front of the TV and watch a documentary about people with rare diseases. No matter how bad things seem, there's always someone who has it worse. Which is quite comforting, even though I don't want anyone to suffer.

"Do we have to watch this?"

"Yes, this evening, we do."

The school gates might as well be the gates to hell. Step inside and someone with horns and a tail will dunk me in warm water and give me eternal wet pants. I assume that nothing particularly nice is going to happen here today, but I can't help smiling as Ada comes toward me.

"Nice to see you," she says, then stops. "What happened to . . . ?" she asks as she puts her hand to her nose.

"Walked into . . . no . . . I didn't walk into anything. August broke it."

"Why did he do that?"

"He turned up at my place with Gabriel and Johnny to check out where I live and to see if my mom is as fat as they say."

"What? They—" she exclaims in a loud voice.

"And then I tried to punch August because he said something horrible about Mom, but I just punched the air. And he didn't."

Ada starts to breathe heavily as she tries to find the right words; her eyes get narrow and flicker. As if she was sad, angry, and desperate all at the same time.

"B-but . . . ," she stammers.

"Yeah, it's all pretty shitty."

"Is there anything I can do? Because it's kind of my fault."

A good question, really. Ada's on the inside. No one would ever think of bothering her. If I could hold her hand, maybe kiss her on the cheek, I think she might even promote me a rank or two. But of course I can't ask anything as crazy as that. But another idea pops into my head. At first it feels evil. But the more I think about it, the more convinced I am that it's suitably evil—and well deserved.

If it works.

"Could you spread a rumor?" I ask.

"Course I can."

"Could you say that Mom is in the hospital?"

"You mean all I have to say is . . . that your mom's in the hospital. Should I say why?"

I think for a moment.

"Say that August pushed her down the stairs."

"What? Did he?"

"Rumors aren't always true. Mom is in the hospital, but not because August pushed her down the stairs. She managed to get there all by herself. August is bound to boast about my nose, but maybe not quite as much if there's a rumor going around that he pushed my mom."

Ada smiles.

"You're not like the others, Bart. I think you're . . ."

"Evil?"

"No, you're just different."

"Is different good?"

"Better than evil."

Ada goes off to spread the rumor and I'm left standing alone on the playground. Everyone who walks past stares at my face, like I was an exhibit or something. I let them look. They'll get used to me walking around with an enormous bandage in the middle of my face soon enough. But right now, I'm headline news.

The bell rings and I head toward the classroom. When the teacher comes in, he spots me immediately. The questions are easy to predict. What happened? Did someone hit you?

Everyone in the class knows I'm lying when I say that I fell when I was dusting the ceiling light.

"Are you sure you should be at school? Because your grandmother called to say that your mother is in the hospital."

I see the reactions all around me. For the rest of the

class, this confirms the rumor that August pushed my mom down the stairs.

"It's fine. I'm going to visit Mom after school."

"But," the teacher starts, "but you can still sing, can't you?"

"Yes, no problem."

It's almost like he heaves a sigh of relief.

"Great. That's good. Excellent. Good. And I hope your mom gets better. Say hello from me. From all of us, actually."

"Will do."

The break is unlike any other. A couple of girls come over and ask how I am. I can't decide between *good* or *bad*, so I say that I can take a lot of pain.

I feel small pangs of guilt whenever I look at August. He started the day in the limelight with his talk of fights and is now standing there with glazed eyes and his hands deep in his pockets. Trying to correct the rumor now would be like pissing in the wind.

Maybe he's frightened that one of the teachers will send him to the principal. Or that a police car will come speeding into the playground. I don't know whether he suspects that I started the rumor or not. He looks in my direction every now and then but doesn't come over.

"It's working."

I hear Ada's voice behind me.

"Thanks."

"I owe you that much."

Then I tell her my plan for the summer show, even though I know that she can't keep her mouth shut about anything. I just need to see how she reacts.

"Sounds like a good idea."

"You really think so?"

She hesitates, thinks about it, and smiles without showing her teeth.

"I just wish you'd sing instead."

After school, I go up to the hospital with Grandma. Mom is sitting up in bed eating a sandwich.

"My lovely boy!" she cries, her mouth full of food. She holds out her arms.

She only just manages to lift her hands up from the bed. I scramble up beside her and we have a long hug. She strokes my back the way she does best and whispers nice things in my ear.

"Do you want the rest of my sandwich?" she then asks.

"No thanks, it's fine."

She wants to know about my day at school. If I've got homework. If I have any plans for the afternoon. Anything I want to watch on TV. She hardly ever asks questions like that normally. Then we're all quiet. The room is white and spotless. Mom is wearing a kind of nightgown that doesn't suit her. Grandma goes out to the bathroom and Mom and I are left with the silence. The window is ajar and sunlight floods half the room. I could say something about the weather.

"Bart," Mom begins.

She's going to say something important. Possibly something about change. Something that she won't be able to follow through.

"Nice weather today, isn't it?" I interrupt.

"Eh, yes, but . . ."

"Just seems to get warmer and warmer every day."

"Listen, Bart."

"I've got a bike."

"You've got a bike?"

"Yes, because I organized the cleanup. So now I have to learn to ride."

And then I tell her about the cleanup. How many people came, and that Grandma is a born leader. Mom smiles at me.

"I know that things can't go on like before," she says. "This has really given me a scare. And now that I'm going to be operated on, to . . . yes, I'm going to have an operation. To make me better. And thinner."

I look out the window. There's a bird in the tree. A sparrow or a thrush, or something else, I'm not sure.

"I have to stop drinking, Bart."

My eyes move from the bird and I look straight into Mom's round face.

"You're going to stop completely?"

Mom has promised a lot of things in the past few years, but never that. She's always had a good reason to go to the bar. A reason that perhaps doesn't sound so good the next morning.

"I'm going to stop drinking altogether. Never get drunk again."

I've never heard her use the word *drink* about anything other than milk and juice. And certainly never heard her use the word *drunk*.

"I know that sometimes I promise more than I can do. But you need a mother who . . . is alive."

"Yeah, they're the best ones."

Mom springs a leak. The tears roll down her cheeks and I look for something to dry them with. I end up using the bedcovers.

"You deserve a better mom, Bart."

"I'm happy with the mom I've got."

"That's a lovely thing to say, Bart. But I should be better. And I'm going to be better."

"There's a bird in the tree," I say, and point.

"I promise."

"Oh, it just flew away."

I sit on the sofa at home and think how stupid it is to make promises you can never keep. When someone on TV talks about peeing in your pants to keep warm, I think about Mom. Not that she pees her pants, but that she's made more promises than she can keep. Will she really do it this time? I decide to believe her. No one is so stupid that they'd do something they know is going to kill them. Especially not my wise, lovely mom.

But if she doesn't keep her promises, I'm leaving. I don't know where I'll go, I'm just going to leave. I'm almost certain of it.

"You're looking very thoughtful," Grandma says.

I stand up and look straight at her, then start to sing. It comes from the very bottom of my belly. The note fills the room before bursting and suddenly cutting through flesh and bone.

Gudleik squawks: *I'm dying, I'm dying!*

I don't go into the bathroom. Instead I run out and I hear Grandma calling my name. Geir is sitting on the stairs, fiddling with something that he then tries to hide when he sees me.

"Hiya, son," he says as something falls out of his hand and down the stairs.

A syringe rolls down onto the next step. The needle is in a sort of plastic casing. He looks up at me before putting it in his pocket. In his other hand, he has a teaspoon and a lighter.

"Can't find the keys to my apartment, you see. Got a bit desperate."

I sit down beside him.

"I'm a bit desperate too," I say.

"*Desperado, oh, you ain't gettin' no younger,*" Geir sings. "*Your pain and your hunger, they're drivin' you home. And freedom, oh freedom well, that's just some people talkin'. Your prison is walking through this world all alone.*"

He hasn't got a great voice, but the song creates a special atmosphere out here on the stairs.

"I love the Eagles," he explains.

"Don't know whether I like them or not. I've only heard you sing them."

"Yeah, yeah, they're better on record. How's the biking going?"

"Thought I'd go for a walk with the bike later on."

"For a walk?"

"Yes, I can't ride a bike."

"Shit, you have to learn to ride a bike, kid."

"Maybe."

"You need a dad, don't you?"

I somehow can't see Mom or Grandma running behind me with a hand on the bike.

"Do you know where you can order one?" I ask.

Geir smiles and shows his rotten teeth.

"No, but if you find a good offer, I'd like to order one too."

"I think mine might have gotten injured in the Iraq War."

"Right."

"Lost both legs."

"Jeez, that's nasty."

Geir knows someone who's lost his legs too. But not in a war. Some of his sores got infected. And then suddenly we're deep in conversation. It jumps around and we stop talking whenever anyone goes past. What makes a police officer okay, the best way to shoplift, what makes good music good. That sort of thing.

Geir is wearing a faded T-shirt that says *All rumors are true*. He's constantly scratching his thighs and neck, with frantic movements.

"Do you know the secret for doing well in life?" he asks out of the blue.

"No."

"Me neither."

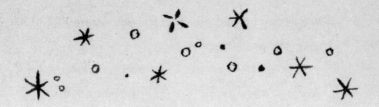

My eleventh chapter

The next morning I get an e-mail from the USA. At first I'm scared it's going to be one of those automatic replies that say we'll contact you later if we can be bothered. I hesitate before opening it. What if it really is the mail I've been waiting for?

I click the mouse with trepidation.

Dear Bart,
    We have been in touch with Mr. John Jones
and are sorry to inform you that he has never
been to Norway and is sure he is not your father.
John Jones is a very common name in the
United States.

We wish you the best of luck in your search
for your father.

Yours sincerely,

Joshua Adams

Publishing Assistant

P.S. Happy birthday!

My dad is out there somewhere and he still has both legs. I guess I'm happy that he doesn't have to walk with false legs for the rest of his life. I google John Jones again and read a little about holy John Jones who lived in the sixteenth century, before I suddenly stumble on a page with contact information for a John Jones who lives in Norway, in a different part of town, but not that far away. What if Dad has moved back to Norway to look for his long-lost son? Now that I have a name and an address, I quickly find a phone number in the telephone directory.

I know. It's stupid to hope. But I can't help it. A bit like when Geir needs just a small dose of heroin, and then he feels great, even though all he really wants to do is quit. Someone on TV said that some people are more prone to addiction. To alcohol. Drugs. Gambling. Or finding their dad. They didn't actually mention that, but I'm sure that it should be on the list.

Let's just say that I check out 365 John Joneses a year. One possible father a day. That's 3,650 John Joneses in the next decade and 7,300 by the time I'm 33. I have no idea how many John Joneses there are in the world, but the name gets enough hits on Google to populate an entire country. Mom said that they met in Oslo, so if I knew how many of them had been in Norway, the search would be a lot easier. Maybe I could get Mom to come to the police so they could draw one of those identikit pictures that I could post on Facebook.

I go into the bathroom and tap in the number with trembling fingers. My heart is thumping pretty wildly. It rings and rings until the voicemail kicks in and a man talks in Norwegian with a heavy American accent. There's something familiar about his voice. As though it were mine, only grown-up.

I'll have to call John Jones again after school.

"I've put a little treat in your lunchbox," Grandma says, and pats me on the head.

"Thank you."

Out in the hall, I open the box and discover three cookies, in addition to a sandwich and a banana. I want to go back and give Grandma a big hug, but there's only nine and a half minutes left until school starts.

Maybe it would be just as good to give up right away. Girls are impossible to understand. And I guess it doesn't get any easier later in life. Ada is waiting for me at the school gates. Like I was someone you'd wait for.

"Why didn't you tell me?" she asks.

"Tell you what?"

"Because you are going to the concert, aren't you?"

"The concert?"

"Yes, he's singing here tonight."

I don't have a clue what she's talking about, and just look like a big question mark.

"You played him to me, Bryn Taffel, or whatever he's called."

"Huh? Bryn Terfel?"

"And I know which hotel he's staying at," she says with a triumphant grin.

"Hotel?"

I'm really trying to understand what's going on. Because I'm not stupid, even if my brain's a bit rusty at times. Bryn Terfel is going to sing this evening. Here in town. Ada knows loads of things I don't know. But why is she talking about his hotel?

"I'm sure there aren't many fans who show up at his hotel. Or what do you figure?"

"How do you know where he's staying?"

"Dad's the director of the hotel chain."

"Oh right."

"Shall we skip class?"

I look at her. I'm guessing I've got the world's stupidest look on my face. But I'm actually trying to get my head around the idea. I can't think of a sensible answer. At least, not until I'm running down the street with Ada. Because that's when I realize that girls really are impossible to understand, and that I shouldn't even try.

"Where's your bag?" I ask when we start to walk again, out of breath.

"At home."

"You planned all this?"

"No one's going to even ask where you were, since your mom's sick."

"And you?"

Ada shrugs.

"Are we just going to show up there?" I ask.

Ada nods.

"But what am I going to say to him?"

147

"You could ask if he's got any advice on how to sing as well when there are people listening."

"He won't have the same problem as me."

"Maybe he did, once upon a time."

Ada goes into a 7-Eleven and buys us both an ice cream. I eat it faster than her, as she talks all the time. When we finally stop in front of the hotel's fancy glass facade, we've both got a bare wooden stick in our mouths.

"We could sit on the bench and see if he comes out," I suggest.

"Three hundred and four."

"What?"

"That's his room number. He might be in his room . . ."

"But . . ."

I feel an iron claw in my stomach. Not unlike the one that sometimes grips me when I have to sing in front of someone else. Of course he won't talk to two wacky Norwegian teenagers. What if he's in the shower and all we get is 100 decibels of rage?

But still, I don't protest when Ada pulls me by the sleeve across the reception area as though we were regular guests. We take the stairs up to the third floor and look at several doors before we find a metal plaque that says 304. I hope that he's anywhere other than in his room. But at the same time, it would be like a dream I didn't know I had coming true. Just the thought of talking to a man with that lung capacity makes my knees weak.

"I don't know if I can speak English," I say.

"Of course you can. I've heard you in class."

"I mean, I don't know if I'll be able to right now."

Ada laughs.

"You know that I can't keep my mouth shut, don't you?" she says. "I can be your interpreter."

And then she does something totally unexpected. She kisses me on the cheek. I don't know whether she thinks that's going to help, but here I am standing outside Bryn Terfel's room being kissed by Ada. Not very surprising, then, that I lose my balance.

"Are you okay?" she asks.

"Yeah, yeah, of course," I reply, leaning against the wall.

She raps on the door. Three hard knocks. I feel like I'm swallowing a dry cloth. She knocks again. Only twice this time. I listen for sounds from inside but hear nothing before the door is suddenly opened.

The man in the doorway is bigger than anyone I've ever seen. I'm not saying that he's the tallest and broadest man in the world, but his silhouette against the sun flooding in through the window behind him makes the Hulk look like a wimp.

"Yes?"

"Are you Bryn Teffel?"

Ada says his name as if he was related to Teflon. I want to kick her in the leg.

"I am."

"This is my friend Bart," she says, pointing at me.

It's good to have the wall for support right now. I try to give him a nod, but my neck has frozen.

"He is a singer, just like you, Mr. Teffel," she continues.

"Good for you," he says, and looks right at me.

He speaks with an accent that I've not even heard in a movie. I know he's from Wales and that he's the son of a farmer. He started singing very young, when a friend of the family taught him Welsh folk songs. Then he trained in London and is one of the best-known bass baritones in the world today. And right now, this great world star is standing in front of me. Is it any wonder that my tongue is tied in knots?

"His voice is better than any I've heard," Ada continues. "But he can't sing in front of people."

"Nervous, are you?" he asks, and looks at me.

"He can speak," Ada informs him.

I nod my wooden neck.

"Come on in."

Then suddenly we're standing in Bryn Terfel's room. I don't know if I should be scared or happy or neither. The hotel room is roughly double the size of our apartment. He's got two suitcases and one is lying open on the bed. It smells of grown man in here. He takes out a couple of cans from a tiny fridge and asks if we want anything.

"A Coke, please," says Ada.

Bryn Terfel looks at me and all I'm capable of thinking is that the voice that I've heard in my ears a million times is coming out of that mouth.

"He will have a Coke too," Ada adds.

I take back a lot of what I've said about Ada. It's good to have her there. Her mouth does what it's supposed to. Not like mine, which either clamps shut or is filled with song and a voice that breaks.

"Can I hear you sing, Bart?" Bryn Terfel asks.

"No," I croak.

I cough a couple of times to clear my throat.

"I thought so. What happened to your nose?"

"I am a boxer."

"You want to box or you want to sing?"

"Sing."

"You know what, there are times in every singer's life when you have serious doubts. For some, that doubt is stronger than for others. Let me show you."

Bryn Terfel throws open the window. He waves to me, and I go over on wooden legs. Then he puts his arm around my shoulders.

"You see the people?"

There are people walking on the sidewalk down below. Lots of people.

"Yes."

"Watch."

The sound is like an explosion inside him. A clear, beautiful explosion. He might as well have had loud-speakers in his mouth. The people on the street stop. Look around. Look up at us. People smile. Bryn Terfel sings so the echoes bounce on the neighboring build-ings. I see how he puffs up his face and forms an *O* with his mouth. And out of his mouth flows the most beauti-ful sound in the universe. After about a minute, he stops abruptly and the people below move on again. Everyone with a smile on their lips. As though they've experienced something special.

"I made a fool out of myself," Bryn Terfel says.

"No, no," I exclaim.

"Who in his right mind would start singing out a hotel window like this? These people think I'm crazy."

"But they were smiling," I say.

"You know, Bart, it was silly to sing out the window. But singing is always a little silly. It does not make world peace. If you start singing like you and I do, we have to be a little crazy. That is the only way we can do it. So tell me, Bart, do you feel crazy enough?"

"I . . . I . . . don't know."

"That's the test. If you can open any window, anywhere, and start to sing, you can do it onstage anytime."

I look over at the window. Will I, who can't even sing properly for my grandmother, ever be able to sing for complete strangers out a window? It sounds impossible. Bryn Terfel smiles at me and pats my head with his great hands.

"It was nice meeting you both. But I have to prepare for tonight's performance. Are you coming?"

I look to Ada for assistance. We should really have a good excuse, but all I have is the truth.

"Eh . . . I didn't know you were singing tonight," I say.

"Listen. Go to the box office and say your name is Bart. There will be two tickets there for you. Okay?"

"Oh . . . eh . . ."

I try really hard to get the words out of my mouth.

"Thank you, Mr. Teffel," Ada says. "We are looking forward to listening more to you."

"Yes, thank you, thank you," I finally manage to add.

Bryn Terfel holds out his hand and pumps my tiny one up and down. Then just as quickly we're back out in the corridor with a can of Coke each. Ada links her arm through mine. Her face is glowing.

"He was so cool!" she says.

"Eh, yes . . . he was, wasn't he?"

"And we're going to the opera!"

"Yes, we are, aren't we?"

Ada is talking so loudly that I pull her away from Bryn Terfel's door. It's as if I've just woken from a crazy dream. Soon I'll realize that I of course never met Bryn Terfel and that I will never see him in concert. But I don't need to pinch myself on the arm. I've got the big man's sweat in my hand.

Ada grins in the elevator and asks: "Have you got anything to say to me?"

"What do . . . oh, yes, thank you."

"You're welcome."

Ada prattles on all the way home and I have problems keeping up with what she's talking about. Bryn Terfel keeps getting in the way, his body and voice spreading out across the town.

I stop. Ada carries on for a few steps, then stops and turns in the middle of saying something about school. I take a deep breath, fill my lungs, and close my eyes. A note steals up my throat and escapes out into the open. And it holds for a quite a while. But then it's as if the sound is cut to shreds with a scalpel.

I open my eyes. Ada comes toward me and says: "You didn't really think you'd manage it the first time, did you? It was a good start, though."

"I will manage to do it," I say, and start to walk again.

"Optimism is good. It makes you live longer."

"It's not optimism. I'm just determined to do it."

When you skip school, it's important not to get home too early. I've never really hung out much in cafés. Mom often says that cafes are places for people who want to be seen. But most of the people around us seem to be more interested in their coffee, newspaper, or conversation than in showing off the latest fashion.

"The others will be doing math now," Ada says.

"I should at least do the homework," I say, and look down at my bag.

Suddenly my phone rings. I don't recognize the number.

"Hello?"

"Who am I talking to?" says a voice with an American accent.

"It's . . . Bart. Who are you?"

"My name is John Jones and someone called me from this number."

I swallow sandpaper and try to make contact with my brain.

"Right. Hi. Yes, I just wondered if you were maybe trying to find a son?"

"What do you mean?"

"My father's name is John Jones."

There's silence at the other end. I expect to hear a click, but nothing happens.

"Hello?" I say.

"I'm here," he replies.

Ada takes my hand. Am I so easy to read?

"I didn't mean to . . . ," I start.

"I don't know."

"You don't know."

"I don't know."

"My mom's name is Linda."

"Perhaps we should meet, Bart?"

Then suddenly I've arranged to meet John Jones tomorrow. The one who doesn't know whether he's my father or not. It can't be ruled out.

"I'm the one with a bandage in the middle of my face," I tell him.

"I'll find you, then."

When I've hung up, I have to tell Ada.

"So it might be him?" she asks.

"I can't quite believe it. Just think how disappointed I'll be if it's not him."

"You're one surprise after the other."

"It's not intentional."

"I've got no surprises."

"Not everyone needs surprises to be interesting. And by the way, I don't really collect pictures of mass murderers."

When I talk to Ada, I never know where the conversation is going to go. Soft, gentle movements one moment, full-frontal attacks the next. Just when I think I understand Ada, she says something that I don't understand at all. What she's saying is not true. She's full of surprises. They're just not the same as mine.

I've cut school today for the first time in my life. And I've got the feeling it won't be the last if I keep hanging out with Ada.

"How was school today?" Grandma asks when I get home.

"I don't know. I went to see Bryn Terfel instead. He sang out his window. And I'm going to see him sing at the opera tonight as well."

"What are you talking about?"

"If that's okay with you?"

Grandma is confused.

"Yes, well, I'm sure it is. Who are you going with?"

"A girl in my class. Ada."

"How exciting."

Then we go to visit Mom. I ask Grandma not to say anything about the concert and my visit to the hotel. Mom is having her operation tomorrow and doesn't need any more worries. While we're talking, she dozes off a couple of times. She doesn't even eat the chocolate that I've brought her.

I'm not even sure that she hears me when I say she's the best mom in the world as I leave. I know that she's actually not the best in the world, but I still think she needs to hear it. And I've only got one mom, and sometimes she can be the best in the world too.

"Should we go to a restaurant?" Grandma asks on the way out.

"McDonald's?"

"No, a real restaurant. Indian, perhaps?"

"I've never had Indian food before."

"Well, let's go to Indian, then."

It's simple to choose at McDonald's or Burger King. The burgers have different names but basically all taste the same. I never get salad or chicken nuggets. But at the Indian restaurant, they've got a whole book of dishes that are hard to say: Murgh Masala, Begum Bahar, and Dhuan Gosht. I go for Tandoori Chicken, because that's what Grandma recommends. We get a flat bread about the size of a pizza that's called naan, lots of rice, and chicken in a little pot. I've never tasted anything like it before. It's spicy, strange, and good.

"Can you afford this?" I ask Grandma.

I don't know if it's the right question to ask, but I'm worried that Grandma's done something stupid.

"Sometimes you just have to put on your big spender jacket."

Grandma's wearing a dress, so I'm not quite sure what she's talking about.

"And you don't need to worry about breakfast tomorrow," she adds.

I meet Ada at the opera house at half past six. She's all dressed up like it was the last day at school.

"My suit's at the dry cleaners," I say.

Ada laughs a little. She knows it's not true.

We go over to the box office, and I say: "My name's Bart."

"That's nice," the woman behind the counter says.

"Um . . . well . . ."

"There should be two tickets for us from Bryn Teffel," Ada explains.

"Terfel," the box office lady corrects her. "You should at least learn to get that right, young lady. Now, let me see, yes, here they are."

She hands us an envelope, and there are indeed two tickets inside.

"Oh no," I say when I look at the tickets. "They've made a mistake. They think we're in the orchestra."

Ada laughs again.

"Orchestra seats, silly. That means we're right down by the front. They're the best seats."

"Obviously I knew that. Do you come here often?"

"We normally come to see *The Nutcracker* before Christmas."

Sometimes I feel like Wolf Boy. The one who grew up with wolves and didn't know how humans lived. Someone who is completely lost when it comes to things that ordinary people know. On the other hand, he could live with wolves. And none of them can.

We go in and sit down in two seats in the middle of the fourth row. Most people are about as old as Grandma, but there are some younger ones too, mainly girls in skirts.

The concert is over within minutes. At least, that's what it feels like afterward. I'm sure I sat with my mouth open the whole time that Bryn Terfel purified my ears and made my stomach tremble. It's one thing listening to him on headphones; it's something else to see his facial expressions, the way his mouth moves, his eyes. How he fills his lungs to bursting before the music pours out of him.

As we leave, Ada tells me that the concert was nearly two hours long. I believe her. She says that it was good, but a bit boring too.

"What? Boring?" I exclaim. "That was boring?"

We get the metro home, and I find it's still hard to have a normal conversation.

"I can kind of see you standing on the stage one day," Ada says.

I lean in toward Ada. I don't know why. After all, she thought it was *a bit boring*. But she smells of melon again.

Tomorrow half the school will no doubt know that we've been to the concert. Sometimes it's not such a bad thing that Ada can't keep her mouth shut.

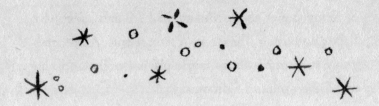

My twelfth chapter

"You'll have to come to the dress rehearsal this evening," the teacher says.

"But I'm going to the doctor about my nose."

"In the evening?"

"Yes, he wants to give it a proper examination. Sometimes splinters of bone get caught in the nasal passages. He was going sailing today, but I said that it was really important to get it checked before the show."

"You're going to close the performance, Bart. It feels rather odd not to know what you're singing."

"It'll be fine. I promise."

I wrote a script about boxing yesterday. At first I thought I'd go through the history of boxing, but that would be too much like a lesson. So instead, I've got lots of funny stories about Muhammad Ali and about why I took up boxing. Three out of ten are true. And there's going to be atmospheric music playing while Christian and Robert mime a fight onstage.

The teacher gives up trying to persuade me to come to the dress rehearsal. I don't know much about nervous wrecks, but the teacher doesn't look too good.

Mom has her operation today. People can die in operations, and doctors can forget to take out the scissors. I should be worrying about things like that. But I'm actually looking forward to it. Looking forward to her waking up again and everything being better.

For the first time in a while, I can actually concentrate in class. Like my brain's come back from vacation.

It doesn't seem like Ada's told anyone about the concert yesterday. I don't know if that's because the music is for wrinklies, or if it's because we went together. And someone might misunderstand.

At break time, I'm left standing on my own. But that's only because no one else is standing where they normally do. That's when I discover that Bertram is part of the circle. He's standing with all the others and that doesn't make sense. Just where I used to stand. Before I have a chance to start worrying about it, something unexpected happens. Ada comes over with three girls and a couple of the boys from Class B. I have to tell myself again: "They're coming over to me!"

What do we talk about? Couldn't tell you. Things that I don't have much practice talking about. Do I really fit in here? I'm sure that some of them are wearing socks that cost more than all my clothes put together.

I cock my head with an expression that says: *Wow, that's interesting, really, you don't say*. It hurts my nose to move my face like that, but what does that matter? The whole time I'm scared that I just look stupid, and that they'll banish me into the outer recesses of the playground. Maybe this is a sick joke?

"I hear you sing opera," one of the boys in Class B says, and everyone turns to look at me.

I guess a quiet yes might have been enough, but somehow it feels a bit mean and impolite.

"If I grow big, not fat, but big and solid, then I might possibly be able to be an opera singer. If I get the kind of voice you can sing out an open window with."

"What, sing out the window?"

"Yes, or anywhere else. But a lot of opera singers sing out open windows. It's something that . . . well, maybe not that many people know."

"Are you taking a window with you to the end-of-year show, then?" the boy wonders.

"No, I'll just stand up straight. Opera singers don't do stage diving or anything like that."

"Certainly not if they're fat."

"No, it would be difficult for the audience to carry them around."

This wasn't going the way I'd hoped. I don't have enough practice with conversations like this. But they're still not laughing at me. They just start to talk about the other things that are going to happen at the summer show. I forget to look interested.

"How's your mom?" Ada asks as we head back into the classroom.

"She's promised that everything will be better from now on."

"Isn't that a good thing?"

"She's promised that before."

"What if she keeps her promise this time?"

"I've thought a lot about it."

We sit down.

"And by the way, I've done my homework for today," Ada says.

* * *

I sit in the café and look at the dads. There are no men of the right age waiting on their own, so I sit down at a table with a good view of the door. It's nearly ten past. Maybe he had to go to an important meeting? Or what if I'm sitting in the wrong place? Maybe I got the time or day wrong? Or he was just joking.

What can you do with a head that's always full of those kinds of questions?

Then something happens that stokes a fire in my stomach. A man comes in the door and looks around the cafe. He's about Mom's age and has a shaved head. He sees me and comes over. I stand up. It should feel like a magical moment. One that you'll remember even when you're old and forgetful.

I don't know whether he looks like me or not. But then I don't know how I'm going to look in twenty-five years' time.

"Are you . . . ?" he asks, and doesn't finish the question because I'm nodding so furiously.

He holds out his hand. A hug somehow seems inappropriate. I have to give it time. We shake hands firmly, then he asks what I would like.

"A hot chocolate, maybe?" I suggest.

He goes over to the counter to get our drinks, and

when he comes back, I secretly pray to myself that he hasn't bought himself a beer. He has my hot chocolate in one hand, and a cup of coffee with froth on top in the other.

"You'll have to tell me your story," he says with his strong American accent.

I give him the short version. The one without the bad bits. Afterward, he pretends to think hard.

"I'm not surprised you want to know," he says. "Let me tell you a bit about myself. I've been in Norway many times. And yes, I was here thirteen to fourteen years ago. I met quite a few girls. Did you say that your mom's name is Linda?"

"Yes," I say, full of hope.

"I don't remember a Linda."

"I think she worked in a bakery."

John Jones shrugs.

"She lived in Tøyen."

He shrugs again.

"She used to ride a red bike with a basket in front."

"She did, did she?"

"And in photographs she's got long, fair hair."

"Did she smile a lot?"

"Yes . . . I think she used to smile a lot."

"I think I remember her."

I don't know why it's taken so long to notice, but John Jones has the same eyes as me. Pale blue and quite deep set.

"And how is . . . Linda?" he asks.

"She's in the hospital. And she doesn't have the red bike anymore. I think she might have changed quite a bit since then."

"Who hasn't?" John Jones smiles and runs a hand over his shaved head.

"It's kind of weird to say this, but I think that . . . you might be my father," I say.

John Jones reaches over the table and pats me on the shoulder. Maybe that's what dads do. A kind of friendly pat rather than a hug.

"There's only one way to be certain," he says. "I have to meet your mom."

"In a couple of days, maybe."

"Perfect. Tell me more about yourself."

How can you summarize thirteen years in half an hour? The strange thing is that I manage. I leave out a whole lot. But I don't lie. I just don't tell him about the bills in the cupboard and the people who live in our building. He doesn't need to know everything at once.

And I ask him about his life as well. And I'm sure he leaves out a lot too, because he only talks for about five minutes. John Jones comes from a town called Texarkana in Texas, but has lived in New York and Washington. He's even lived in London and Paris for a while. But something has always drawn him back to Norway, and he can never put his finger on what. I think that maybe it's the suspicion that he might have a son here. But I don't say that out loud.

John Jones works with computers and doesn't have a girlfriend. He likes going to the races and hiking in the mountains in summer.

"Do I have any . . . half brothers or sisters . . . that you know of?"

"No."

"Do you like opera?"

"Funny you should ask. Not really, but I did go to see Bryn Terfel at the opera."

"You were there? So was I."

"Wow! Great! Wasn't it fantastic?"

"It was . . . really great. But . . ."

The word *dad* is on the tip of my tongue. I so want to say it. I've always wanted to say it. Like it was some rare word that was only used on special occasions. Instead, I tell him about Bryn Terfel singing out the window, and John Jones laughs. My dad has a nice laugh.

"Do you like cycling?" he asks out of the blue.

"I just got a bike," I tell him, but don't say that I only push it around at the moment.

"I like biking as well," he says. "Maybe we could go for a ride."

We decide that I'll call him and that we'll go to the hospital to see Mom. Everything is going to be fine. Maybe Mom and Dad will get back together again? I've read on the Internet about couples who get back together fifty years after they first met. It would only be thirteen years for Mom and Dad. Thirteen years is nothing.

Before we go, he asks: "What happened to your nose?"

"Someone said horrible things about my mom."

"Bart, I really like you."

"The operation went well," Grandma tells me when I get home.

"That's fantastic. Right now things are going well in my life too."

"Oh, I'm so pleased, Bart."

"I'm a little scared, though. Scared it won't continue."

"Of course it will, Bart. Things will continue to be good, because you deserve it."

Where do grandmothers come from? It's as if grandmothers are put on this earth to smooth things out when life gets rough. I've read that the king presents a medal to people who have done something special in their time. I think all grandmothers should get a medal like that. A special grandmothers' prize.

She helps me take the bandage off my nose. It's not quite straight, but you'd need a level to spot it. My nose is still swollen and it hurts every time she touches the nose bone. There's still a scab on a cut at the tip. I look like myself again without the bandage. With an almost normal face, I feel ready for new challenges.

"I'm going to learn to ride a bike today," I say with determination.

"Your mom used to like biking," Grandma says.

"She had a red bike with a basket on the front when she met Dad. Can you remember it?"

"I certainly do."

I go out and unlock my bike. Two wheels, handlebars, pedals, and a frame. How hard can it be? I'm too old for training wheels, so I'm just going to have to risk blood and bruises. If I can get up enough speed, I'm sure the balance thing will sort itself out.

I get onto the saddle and can only just reach the pedals with my feet. Hands on the handlebars, a quick check of the brakes. The sun is shining on the road. If I think I'm going to fall, I will. I have to convince myself that I can ride. I'm going to bike down the street without any trouble. Pedal until I feel my thighs ache.

It's time for my first bike ride.

I'm about to push off when I hear someone shuffle up behind me.

"You can't ride like that."

Geir's eyes are glazed and his knees are extra bendy.

"Oh, hi. What am I doing wrong?"

"You're leaning too far forward. You'll just tip over. Have to look up and see where you're going, not look down at the ground."

He holds on to the frame.

"Right, sit straight now. Then put one foot down on the pedal. That's right, yeah! I'll run behind you. Come on! Give it some!"

I ride. Even though the front wheel wobbles and I try to compensate by moving my butt to keep the balance, I roll off down the street. Geir is holding me. At least, I think he is until I'm suddenly lying on the pavement and discover that he's far behind me.

"Cool! You can bike, dude."

"Weren't you going to hold on?"

"I held on for a couple of steps, but can't run, you see. My feet are messed up."

I've got a graze on one hand, but nothing serious. I kept my nose well off the ground. And anyway, I've ridden a bike and don't intend to give up now. I get back up onto the saddle.

"Imagine my invisible hand on the frame!" Geir shouts.

And so I do just that. I imagine Geir behind me, stopping me from falling down.

Okay, I fall over a couple of times and eventually get a rip in my pants and the blood trickles down my leg, but soon I'm wobbling around on the bike without falling over. My body works with the two wheels and the frame. I can go biking with Dad. Geir claps and cheers me on.

"I think I might have found my dad," I tell Geir as I weave in a circle around him.

"Cool. Has he got legs?"

"Two. And he's from Texas. So half of me is from Texas."

"Very cool. I like ZZ Top. Has he got a long beard? Cowboy hat? Bolo tie?"

"Um, no, he's quite . . . normal."

"Good, good. The normal ones are usually the best."

"I like him."

"Then I like him too."

I ride some more and only fall off one more time. I think that means I can bike.

"That's freedom," Geir says, and puts his hand on the frame. "You can go where you like now. People go around the world on these. Just watch that someone like me doesn't steal it."

"I promise I'll look after it."

Grandma cleans the cut on my knee and says that she'll fix my pants. She's changed the bed and found the envelope of mass murderers with Ada's name on it under the mattress.

"Should I be worried?" she asks.

"I can't promise that I'll never embarrass you. But I can promise that I'll never be a mass murderer."

I send Dad a text to ask if he can come to the hospital tomorrow at four. He answers immediately: *Yes. See ya.*

So it's not biking that I think about when I go to bed. Tomorrow is such an important day that I should be feeling like a jellyfish. But I'm perfectly calm as I lie there looking up at the ceiling. Everything is going to be all right. This is the end of the hard times.

And no doubt there's a beautiful, real shooting star outside the window.

The day starts perfectly. Grandma makes pancakes for breakfast. She's bought bacon and maple syrup. I let my crispy bacon pancakes drown in the yummy brown syrup.

"As long as you eat this afterward, it's fine," she says, and puts a red apple beside my plate.

I get up and give Grandma a hug. Cool kids don't hug their grandmothers, I know. But I can't help it.

"It's going to be a great day," I say.

"Of course it's going to be a great day," she repeats.

Someone has dropped a whole lot of advertising by the mailboxes out in the hall, and there's a bag of trash on the stairs that has split open. But it doesn't matter, I can organize another cleanup.

When I walk into the playground, Ada appears.

"The dress rehearsal yesterday went well," she says. "The teacher thinks it's going to be the best show ever."

"So he doesn't need my finale?"

"Yes, he does. He played a recording by some opera

singer in the end, and he cried. It's true. He's expecting something major."

"You don't think he'll be as touched by the boxing?"

Ada shrugs. "I promise, I haven't told anyone. So maybe I can keep secrets after all."

My plan immediately feels stupid. People who cry when they hear singing are not often moved by seeing people pummel each other. My only chance is if the audience likes it. My plan is to finish the whole thing off by commentating the fight between Christian and Robert with great enthusiasm. In the end, Christian will knock Robert out and I'll count to ten while he's down. Then I hope there will be cheers and stamping, at least thunderous applause.

The first thing the teacher says when I come into the classroom is: "I'm looking forward to this evening."

"Me too," I say.

I've got blisters on my vocal cords! A cute squeaky voice! Heart in my throat! I'm sure there are plenty of ways to explain to him that I can't possibly sing this evening. Explanations that mean I have to move somewhere else, immediately.

In the break, I check my cell phone and see that there's a new message from John Jones. *Look forward to seeing you again. John,* it says. That's the kind of thing good dads write. The sort you can rely on, who change their children's lives. If Ada wasn't standing beside me talking all the time, I would probably have thought more about Dad. I just manage to follow what she's saying, and squeeze in some *really*s and *no way*s to show that I'm listening.

I'm on two different planets in class. I'm on the class-room planet, but then sometimes pop over to my own world, where only I know what's going on. The teacher asks me to read and I know more or less where we are in the book, even though I was just traveling between planets.

It's like the whole class has ants in their pants. No one can sit still and the room is full of whispers and notes being passed around. Wouldn't surprise me if no one hears a word of what I'm reading.

Ada walks some of the way home with me, even though she lives in the opposite direction.

"Do you want to go for a bike ride one day?" I ask.

"Where?"

"Maybe somewhere where we can swim?"

"Isn't the water still a bit cold?"

"Or in the forest?"

"Yeah, we could go to the forest."

"Or along the road somewhere."

"Maybe a road to the forest?"

"But don't you have to have one of those mountain bikes if you're in the forest?"

"Probably better."

"Might be better to stick to the road, then."

"Okay, we can bike on the road."

"That'd be nice."

Before she turns back, she gives me a high five and says that it's going to be a cool evening, or something like that.

"Yeah, it's going to be cool."

With Bryn singing in my ears, I read the boxing manual. When I turn the corner by the kiosk, I stop in my tracks. There's a flashing blue light reflected in the windows of our building. And a yellow ambulance by the entrance. It's been here before. Every time I feel my heart in my throat.

Has something happened to Grandma?

I pull out Bryn and run to the building. The ambulance crew are just maneuvering the stretcher into the back. Cheap Charlie is standing by the door, holding back an angry man I've never seen before.

"You bastard!" the man shouts. "Don't you die on me now."

Cheap Charlie has a firm grip on him and stops him from getting to the person on the stretcher.

"You owe me money, you scumbag!"

Even though he's shouting, there's something familiar about his voice that sends a shiver down my spine.

"You're not going to die on me this time, Geir!" he shouts.

I catch sight of the person on the stretcher. It's my Geir. Geir who taught me to bike, who can't die now when I've just gotten to know him.

"Don't you die before I've got my money!" the man screams.

It's like my heart is doing somersaults in my throat. I get to the ambulance just before they shut the door. Geir is lying on the stretcher with a white face and closed eyes. His T-shirt that says *All the rumors are true* has been ripped to shreds.

"What's wrong with him?" I ask.

"Overdose," the paramedic tells me. "Are you family?"

"Me? No. Will he live?"

"Watch out now."

He closes the door and then gets in behind the wheel. In a minute they're driving down the street, the siren blaring.

Cheap Charlie lets go of the shouting man.

"You know what?" the angry man says to Cheap Charlie. "I was told that Geir was dead. And he's alive. And now he might die again. Talk about unlucky!"

"Idiot," Cheap Charlie says, and goes in.

Now I know where I've heard the voice before. It was the angry man who thought Geir lived in our apartment, and it was me who told him that Geir was dead. I slip in through the door behind Cheap Charlie.

"Was it you who found him?" I ask.

"No, it was that nut out there," Cheap Charlie says, nodding toward the angry man. "He tried to bring him around by hitting him. It's all about money—no one cares about people anymore."

"Will Geir live?"

"I don't know. But those people are experts in keeping people like Geir alive. It's not the first overdose he's taken."

"Do you think anyone will visit him in the hospital?"

"Believe me, he won't be expecting anyone."

Cheap Charlie goes into his apartment. I stay where I am out in the hallway. There's a syringe on the floor, full of light red liquid. I pick it up and hurl it against the wall.

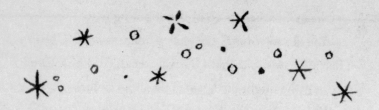

My thirteenth chapter

"When does the thing at school start?" Grandma asks.

"It's the end-of-year show. And it starts at six."

My voice is flat. Not as in off-key, but as in depressed and angry. Grandma comes over and runs her hand through my hair.

"Are you nervous? Is that what it is?"

I don't want to answer. The new honest me will say more than it's good for a grandmother to know. I haven't told her that Dad's going to show up at the hospital either. I hope he remembers to bring flowers.

"It's important that we're at the hospital at exactly four o'clock," I say.

"So we can get to the show on time?" Grandma asks as she folds some clothes.

"That too. But Grandma, have you . . . have you ever wondered who my dad is?"

"It's never been that important to me. But I understand if it's important to you. Remember, lots of children grow up without ever seeing their dad. It's not that unusual these days, and they still turn out well."

"But what if Dad suddenly showed up one day. Would you be happy?"

"Yes, if he was a good dad. Your mom's not very well at the moment . . . so yes, he might come in handy."

There's a ring at the door. Grandma and I look at each other.

"Are you expecting anyone?" she asks in a hushed voice.

I shake my head. Grandma points at the peephole and I look through. There's a woman standing outside who I think I've seen before, but I can't place her. Then I see another face, lower down. One that I definitely recognize. I feel my stomach lurch, and can't open the door.

"Who is it?" Grandma asks.

Instead of explaining, I take a deep breath, and reluctantly push down the door handle. The next second I'm looking straight into a very unhappy face.

"Hi, August," I say.

"Hi," he replies.

"Are you . . . ?" his mom asks when she sees Grandma.

"I'm his grandmother."

"Oh, of course. His mother's . . ."

"In the hospital."

"Of course, yes. August has something to say to you."

August looks at the floor. This version of August doesn't even resemble the one I meet at school every day. His mother has her hand on his shoulder.

"Sorry that I punched you," August says in a small voice.

"That's okay," I say, and hope that he'll leave right away.

"I just have to ask about something," his mom says hesitantly.

I hope that Grandma doesn't ask them in for coffee and cookies.

"Is it true that August pushed your mother, or rather, your daughter, or . . . didn't he?"

"What do you mean?" Grandma says.

"He didn't push her," I cut in.

"Okay. So why is everyone saying that August pushed her?"

I could say *I don't know*. Maybe even tell her that's what it's like to be a mom. Everyone is subject to rumors now and then. And sometimes they're not true. That's why they're called *rumors*. She can't make her son popular again. There's lots of us at the bottom of the ladder. Welcome to our world. But you can survive down here too.

But then I think of something. Since no mom wants to think badly of her child, it's a risky strategy. But I can't stop myself.

"Because I started the rumor," I explain.

"B-but why?" August's mom stammers.

"Because otherwise August would have boasted about breaking my nose and I would have to deal with all sorts of problems. But because everyone thinks he pushed Mom, he stopped bragging about breaking my nose."

Perhaps I should say something about August being a leader, someone who takes up a lot of room, and who others listen to. I could even say that he's not always horrible, sometimes he's actually quite nice, especially to his friends. Then it hits me: What if August and I could be friends? How crazy would that be?

"Is that true?" August's mom looks at him.

"I've got a suggestion," I say before August can answer. "If August and I can be friends, I'll stand up in class and say what actually happened to Mom."

"So you're not friends?" his mom says, and looks at August again.

"I'm not really friends with any of the boys in the class," I continue. "They generally act as if I don't exist. I don't mean that he has to come here or that we should be best friends. Just act friendly, really."

August's mom doesn't ask any more questions. A hand is held out feebly in front of me. It belongs to August.

"Deal," he says.

I take his hand before his mom has a chance to say anything.

"So, that's everything sorted out?" Grandma asks.

"Yes, I guess it is," August's mom replies.

Grandma and August's mom say the sort of things that polite adults do. I notice that his mom is craning her neck to get a look into the apartment, to get an impression of our slum. No parents want their children to be friends with people who live in a cockroach nest, but she realizes this is the only deal that can save August right now. He's got a smart mother. Behind us, Gudleik cackles: *Help, I've got nothing to wear.*

When they've gone, Grandma asks me if it was all true.

"Yes."

"It's been a long time since I was at school, I suppose."

I stare out the tram window on the way to the hospital. Dad, Geir, and the show—it should all be wreaking havoc with my nerves. But my eyes are as empty as a gym after school. I can't get my thoughts in order. I'm sure there are buildings and people, dogs and cars passing by outside the window, but I can't seem to focus on anything. It's almost like I can't see.

"You're very quiet," Grandma says.

I smile at her. This could still be the best day of my life. I have to focus on that.

As we walk up to the hospital from the tram, I ask: "Is it okay if I go in to see Mom on my own today?"

"If you'd like to, yes."

"You could come in a bit later. But I just want to talk to her a little . . . first."

"Of course you can. I'll sit outside and enjoy the sun."

Suddenly I've got a knot in my stomach. I shouldn't lie to Grandma. But I haven't got the headspace to answer all her questions if I tell her about Dad.

Grandma finds a bench and sits down. When I get

to the entrance, I can see him walking around in a kind of circle inside. Dad has his arms full of flowers.

"Hi," I say, and don't know if I should hug him or not today either.

He seems to be just as uncertain, so we shake hands again. He starts to talk about how hard it was to know which flowers to buy, so he got all kinds. Apparently flowers can mean lots of things—some are best for funerals, others say *I love you*, and he just wanted to get something nice and ordinary that didn't mean anything in particular.

"They look lovely," I say when he's talked too long about the flowers.

Dad's face is all sweaty. He brushes something off his shirt and blows his nose, making his cheeks red.

Up on the ward, I'm told she's in Room 117. We agree that Dad should wait outside. I walk quietly into the room and see that Mom's awake. When she sees me, she says *hello* in a happy but tired voice. No matter how hard she tries, she can't hide how exhausted and weak she is.

"How did the operation go?" I ask.

"It went well. I'm going to get back in shape, lose weight, and then I should be able to work more. And then, Bart, we'll move."

"Maybe it's best to take one thing at a time."

"If I can get a permanent job, then we can rent a better apartment in another area. Just say where you want to live."

I sit down on the edge of the bed.

"Mom, I was wondering."

"Yes?"

"You know Dad. John Jones. I've sort of been looking for him."

"Oh, Bart, my lovely boy. It's such a common name."

"But what if . . ."

"I understand that you want to find him. But you'll only be disappointed. Can't you promise me not to . . ."

I stand up and stop Mom in midsentence.

"Hang on," I say, and rush over to the door.

I wave at Dad, who comes into the room slowly, holding the flowers in front of him like a shield. Mom looks at me with knitted, skeptical eyebrows.

"Hello again," he says, and puts the flowers down on the bed.

Even though she's tired after the operation and no doubt pumped full of pills, she straightens up and pulls away slightly from Dad.

He holds out his hand and says: "I'm John Jones. I believe we have . . . met before."

Mom looks like she's seen a ghost. She doesn't take his hand, just looks at me with shocked eyes.

"Who is this?" Mom asks seriously.

"This is . . . Dad . . . ," I reply.

I almost add *I think*, but I so badly want to convince Mom that it's him. People change. There could be a thousand reasons why she doesn't recognize him right away. Just wait until he tells you about the red bicycle. Yes, John Jones is a common name, but not in Norway. It's an unusual name here!

"I'd like a word with you, Bart," Mom says.

John Jones stays standing where he is.

"He's brought you flowers," I try.

"Should I . . . ?" Dad asks, and nods toward the door.

"Yes, could you give us a few minutes?" Mom asks.

John Jones walks toward the door. I want to ask him to stay, so that Dad can hear what we're talking about. He's part of the family. I know it's all a bit much for Mom. It was stupid of me to think she'd be happy to see him. Especially when she's so weak. What do I know, maybe they fought all the time. Maybe John Jones ran off with another woman.

"Come here," Mom says, and pats the sheet beside her.

"I'm fine here, really."

"Where did you find him?" she asks in a grave voice.

"On the Internet."

"I always knew you'd look for him one day. But I thought you'd tell me you were looking, and then I could ask you not to."

"But I've found him. He's standing outside the door. His name is John Jones. He remembers your red bicycle with the basket in front."

"His name is not John Jones."

"But he told me his name is . . . What do you mean?"

"Your dad's name is not John Jones. I made that up."

The room was suddenly very small and claustrophobic. I back away from Mom a few steps.

"But he . . . he said . . ."

"The truth is that I can't really remember who your father is. It was at a time when I was drinking quite a lot, and . . ."

"He remembers your red bicycle," I say in a feeble voice.

"I don't think it's him. I'm sorry."

The words are like an echo in my head. *I'm sorry* bounces around and around inside my skull like a bouncy ball.

"I made up John Jones because it was foreign, and

I thought it was such a common name that if you ever did start to look, you'd give up very quickly. I'm afraid I remember absolutely nothing about your father. I'm so sorry, Bart."

"But what if . . ."

I don't say any more. The percentage chance that the man outside the door is my father is so miniscule that it shouldn't be calculated. No one cares about such small numbers.

Mom attempts a smile. She holds out her hand. I'm right over by the wall. It feels cold against my arms. I suddenly realize that John Jones is actually just a sad man who can't remember all the women he's been with. Someone who wishes that he could find a forgotten son who needs him. A boy who could give his life meaning. A life that hasn't turned out the way he hoped it would.

I run out. Mom calls after me in a weak voice. I stop in front of John Jones.

"It was really nice of you to want to be my dad. But apparently you're not, after all," I say, and hurry on down the corridor.

"But . . . but it was nice meeting you," John Jones says behind me. "And I'm sorry . . . but I don't remember your mom."

I clatter down the stairs at full speed and find Grandma sitting on the bench outside.

"You can go up now," I say.

"Where are you off to?"

"I'm going to school."

"Shouldn't we go together?"

I'm already racing toward the tram.

I head to the playground. Today can still turn out well. No days are all bad. I just have to dig deep enough. Even if this is not my day, I might still find a little gold nugget. Or something else that glitters.

All the people I pass are happy. Some have won a soccer match. Met a good friend. Found their father.

Then there I am standing on the playground. There's no one here. The school could be any old, empty building. As I stand there staring at the building, I think of more death. Because this is not where I should be. I should be visiting Geir in the hospital. If he's alive. No wonder thinking makes people depressed.

"Good that you could come early," says a voice behind me.

I turn around and look straight into our teacher's smile.

"Oh, hello."

"All well with the voice?"

"Yes, it's good."

"I just wanted to ask . . . ," the teacher starts, obviously looking for the right words. "That recording, well, it is you singing, isn't it?"

"Yes."

"Great. I just wanted to be sure. Since you weren't there yesterday."

"But . . . what if . . ."

Now it's me who's lost for words. They seem to slip away so easily.

"Yes?"

"What do you think about boxing?"

"Boxing? Well, I've got nothing against boxing. Why do you ask?"

"Well . . ."

My cell phone starts to play a tune and vibrate in my pocket. I fish it out and see that it's Christian calling.

"I have to take this," I say, and walk away from the teacher, who nods and walks toward the school.

"Hello, it's Bart."

"Hi, Bart. What's up?"

"I'm at school."

"Cool. Mega cool. That's good," he says, then hesitates. "Listen, something's come up."

"Something's come up?"

"Yeah, it turns out that Robert's got to sort out some family drama, and I can't box on my own."

"You have to come!"

"I know it stinks. But I don't think it's going to work."

"But . . . but then I don't have anything."

"I'd just make an idiot of myself. But if anyone messes with you, I'll come and give them one. Promise."

My mouth is completely dry. If I had money, I'd give it all to Christian now.

"But Christian . . ."

"And I've got a date."

"Oh . . . right."

We say good-bye and hang up. I'm standing alone on the playground, and right now, this asphalt square is a whole alien country. Cars pass outside on the road. I hear people talking on the sidewalk. Some children are shouting in the distance. I'm the only person in my country.

No one wants a country all to themselves.

I look up at the school building. It's bigger than I remember. I don't like this school. It's far too big and in your face.

I cross the playground and go in the same door as the teacher. Then I walk down the corridor and go up to the second floor. I open a window out to the street as wide as it will go. There's a woman walking past outside with a stroller, some boys biking toward the school, and a man hobbling with a stick toward the store.

I draw a deep breath, deep, deep. The music comes from way down inside my body. The sound pours out of my throat. The volume is screwed up to the max. The people turn and look toward the school. They spot me in the window. I sing at the top of my voice, and the sound crackles a little at the edges. Then something happens. And it happens very suddenly. As if a machete has sliced the song to pieces and all the sounds collide.

The boys on the bikes laugh. The woman with the stroller hurries on. Only the old man stays there listening to my noise pollution. I stop. There's no point in continuing.

"Bart," says a voice that I know only too well, behind me.

"What?" I say, without turning around.

"Well, I heard you . . . singing," the teacher finishes.

"Mm."

"Perhaps you shouldn't close the concert after all."

"Maybe not."

"It'll be fine. We can manage with what we've got. It'll be a great end-of-year show."

"It was me singing in the recording."

"Yes, of course it was, but . . . There will be a lot of people in the auditorium, and well . . ."

"I don't need to be part of it."

He comes over to me and puts a hand on my shoulder. The way grown-ups do when they want to comfort you. But right now, a hand on my shoulder is not enough. I shrug it off and he lets go.

"I'll find a way to explain to the others why you're not going to sing. Leave it to me. No one will be angry with you."

I close the window and turn around. And see immediately that there's someone else standing behind the teacher. Ada does not look happy. Like something terrible has happened. Then I realize she's unhappy because of me. The boy who can't sing for anyone other than toothbrushes and the medicine cabinet.

She comes over to me and takes my hand.

"Are you . . . ?" the teacher asks.

We both shake our heads at the same time.

"Sing again," Ada says quietly. "Just close your eyes."

Her hand is warm. The moment I close my eyes, the teacher doesn't exist. I think I hear Ada whisper *It's all right* beside me, but I'm not sure.

"And this means . . . what's . . ."

I shut out the teacher's stammering, take a few deep breaths, and hold for a second, two, three. As I hold on to the oxygen, I have time to think that this is probably a bad idea. At the same time I realize that I'm no longer standing in the school with a stressed-out teacher. And I'm not in the bathroom at home. I'm standing on a stage in front of hundreds of people. And I'm about to sing.

The sound wells up in me. My voice is like a helmet around my head. Ada squeezes my hand. I think it's because she's happy. The acoustics are fantastic on this stage. Almost like a spacious corridor. I sing with everything I've got.

Alone.

On the stage.

It leaves me breathless. Ada lets go of my hand. I open my eyes, and at first there is silence. The teacher is standing closer to me now than when I closed my eyes.

"That was . . . that was quite . . . well, just . . . ," he stutters.

"It was fantastic," Ada whispers.

"Yes, yes, fantastic. Do you get very nervous?" the teacher asks.

"That's the first time I've ever managed to sing for anyone," I tell him.

"Would you manage onstage . . . if Ada was holding your hand?" he asks.

I really want to say: *Yes, her warm hand fixes everything*. But I can't see into the future today either.

"I don't know."

"Okay. Let me put it this way: Shall we risk it?"

"It might look a bit weird if I hold Ada's hand onstage," I say, and look over at her.

"Yes, maybe," the teacher says, all excited. He rubs his temples as he thinks. "But there's a curtain. Listen. Why don't you stand behind the curtain, holding Ada's hand, so you can't see the audience. All the people who've performed can go out in front of the curtain, one by one, and then, right at the end, when you've almost finished the song, we can raise the curtain. It will be brilliant— no one will have seen a finale like it."

Being negative doesn't make life any better. I've always thought that I'll get by if I can be positive. Right now, I see possibilities. I can sing. It could work. If I refuse to think that anything might go wrong, well then there's no chance of it all going badly wrong.

I think that's logical, in a weird way.

"Okay."

The teacher hugs me. Which feels weird as well. Then he rushes off down the stairs.

"I think he's crying again," Ada says.

It's quite chaotic backstage before the show. It's been decided that Class B will open the show, and they're doing their final preparations while Class A are sitting around in small groups. The place is heaving with nerves, singing, and warm-ups. I do nothing. Just sit there leaning against the edge of a table. There must be some kind of electricity in the air, only I'm not plugged in. Apparently, people who freeze to death get warm again just before they die. That's me. I'm in the final phase. My nervousness has advanced to numbness. I breathe, swallow, and can hold my hand out without it shaking. There must be something that's not right.

Ada is going to dance and is wearing some kind of hip-hop outfit. Bertram has a whole lot of chains around his neck. August says hello and asks how my voice is.

"Fine, I think."

"It'll be cool to hear you sing."

"It'll be cool to hear you . . . what are you doing?"

"I'm doing a couple of sketches with Gabriel and Johnny."

The teacher is all red in the face and asks people the same question a thousand times. He double-checks all the technical equipment and peeps out at the audience through the curtain.

Why is my inner fire not burning? How come I can still move my arms and legs? My mouth should be drier than the Sahara. The only thing I know is that I should be petrified. Scared that this is the worst idea in the world, and that the magic that happened out there on the stairs will never happen again.

If you compare that with the thought of Mom getting better or Geir surviving, it's nothing more than a scab. It doesn't even hurt. There's no blood.

Maybe that's what it is? There are too many things going on in my life that are far more important than this.

I look at the others. Some of them are practicing, others joking around, nearly all of them talking. Class A have been told that the finale has changed. The teacher will direct it all, and everyone has to line up and do exactly what he says. No one has asked me why it's changed. Maybe they think it's normal that things like this change at the last moment.

It's only an end-of-year show. And kind of the end of the world.

My cell vibrates on silent, and even though it's not great timing, I answer it.

"Hi, it's John Jones."

"Oh, hi."

He clears his throat.

"I just wanted to say that it would be nice if we could still go for that bike ride."

I'm about to tell him that I've just learned to ride, but instead I parrot him like an idiot: "Bike ride?"

"Or something else."

"Or something else?"

"Yes, hang out, you and me. Even though I'm not your dad. I just thought that it might be nice."

I don't answer.

"It's quite all right if you don't want to," he adds.

There's a faint humming on the line. The voices and sounds around me. The seconds tick by.

"I understand," says John Jones, the man who's not my father.

Nice. The word shouts out somewhere in my brain.

"It was nice knowing you," he continues, and I expect to hear a click on the other end at any moment.

"Nice," I say loudly.

"What?"

"I said nice."

"Oh, right. Yes, it was . . . nice."

"You can never be my dad."

"I know."

"But it would be . . . nice if we could maybe be friends."

"I like going to cafés and the movies and theme parks."

"I think I do too. But I kind of haven't done it much."

"I've never been to that amusement park Tusenfryd, either. Maybe we could bike there. I'll call one day. Okay?"

"Okay."

"Break a leg in the show."

"Thank you."

There's still hope for today. It might still go down in the history books as something not completely hideous and awful. The kind of day you remember when you're sitting in the old folks' home. If you try really hard.

Class B get a standing ovation for their part of the show. Then the Class A-ers do their turns one by one.

There's juggling, magic, dancing, music, and yoyo tricks, and August and his buddies get everyone howling with laughter. The whole time I'm sitting backstage on the edge of a table, watching the others getting nervous just as they go onstage, then coming off again happy. The teacher's on fire with this crazy grin on his face that beams success. We're a whole league above Class B.

"That was such fun," Ada says, out of breath, when she comes over after she's danced.

"I didn't see you," I admit, and am a bit worried that she'll tell me that I'm self-centered.

If she said that, I'd just say it was true. Of course I should have watched her and given her heaps of compliments when she came off the stage. What kind of a friend am I?

"I once read somewhere that nerves make you more alert and energetic," Ada says. "People who make a fool of themselves onstage don't have that extra charge going through them. You are a bit nervous, aren't you?"

"I . . . don't know."

"It'll be fine."

And then I see that Ada's got makeup on. I haven't noticed until now. Her lips are extra red and there's something dark around her eyes. Her skin looks more matte than usual. It's like looking at a picture of a more grown-up Ada. Girls are frightening. Fantastic and frightening.

"Five minutes to go," the teacher says to me as he jogs past on his way over to Bertram, who is about to go onstage.

Ada sticks close as the seconds fly by. When the teacher says "one minute," I don't know where the other four went.

I stand up. It's going to happen. Now. I try to breathe normally. And then I realize: I'm nervous. Everything's going to be all right. I am clear and alert.

Before I get to the stage, the teacher comes over and says: "Bart, we've got a problem."

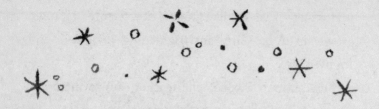

My final chapter
(don't worry, I don't die)

The others crowd around Bertram and slap him on the back with great admiration. Two girls from the class are onstage singing a Beyoncé song on playback. The teacher towers over me, talking. I'm not sure I understand what he's saying. But I know what it means.

"So what do we do now?" he asks.

As if I know how to solve a stage crisis.

"Eh, I don't know," I say.

The curtain won't close. The janitor was meant to fix it ages ago. The mechanism has been sticky for years. It had to happen sooner or later. And now the curtain won't budge.

"Okay, okay, okay," the teacher says, rubbing his face. "We can resolve this."

The girls onstage are singing the last verse.

"Should we stand together onstage?" Ada asks. "I don't mind."

The whole class is gathered around me. They were supposed to go out on the stage as I sang. One after the other. The cherry on the cake. Everyone's looking at me.

I swallow a brick.

There's applause from the audience. The girls bounce offstage. My vision is blurred; the others are just a shapeless mass. But my voice is clear when I say: "I'll go onstage."

Ada clasps my hand.

"Alone."

She lets go.

"Are you sure?" the teacher asks in a strangled voice.

"Do you want to stand here and discuss it?"

"Play the music!" he shouts, before he mumbles: "And may the Lord be with us."

Someone hands me a microphone. I mount the three steps onto the stage, and seeing all the people in the audience is a bit of a shock. Their eyes are glued to me. I spot Grandma in the front row. She gives me a strained smile and clasps her hands, as if she's praying to the teacher's Lord that I won't shame the family for all eternity.

The music flows out of the speakers and I know that I mustn't think that something might go wrong. If I do, I'll only drive knives into the ears of the audience.

Too late. I've already thought it.

There's no point in closing my eyes. I've seen all their peering eyes. Fortunately, a couple of spotlights come on and I'm blinded. A few more bars, and then glorious sound will emerge from my mouth.

Suddenly I see Dad. Not John Jones, but my real dad. He's sitting on his own in the auditorium waiting for me to start singing. Dad sends me an encouraging smile. His hands aren't folded. He's totally calm.

Of course I can sing for Dad.

I take a deep breath. And then I open my mouth.

I'm lying on a floor. I look up into a spotlight. There are sounds all around me. Someone takes hold of me. I'm lifted up, even though all I want to do is stay lying on the floor. The safe, solid floor.

Dad's disappeared. The auditorium is full of other people again. They're all standing. Is that so they can see what's happened? Did I faint? Did I ruin everything?

Everyone is moving their hands in a way I've seen a

thousand times before. Are they clapping for me because I'm alive?

"You did it, you did it!" the teacher shouts too loudly in my ear.

Did what?

The rest of the class are standing around me onstage. They bow. I lower my head and just about fall to the floor again, but someone holds me up. Grandma is whooping like she's at some rock concert. It's embarrassing, but great at the same time.

We leave the stage, then go back on again. The teacher doesn't even try to hide the fact that he's crying. And when we finally file offstage again, he gathers everyone around him.

"You know what? This is . . . this is the best . . . the very best thing that has ever happened to me as a teacher. And it's thanks to all of you," he says in a voice that's barely recognizable.

And then he hugs me. Only me. For a long time.

I gently try to extract myself and then take a few steps back from the teacher, who dries his tears on his sleeve. Ada comes over, grinning.

"Don't think anyone's gotten to smell the teacher's armpits before," she says.

"Ada," I start, then stop. "Did I . . . sing okay?"

"You sang better than you did on the stairs. Surely you could hear that yourself?"

"I . . . I can't remember singing. I only remember Dad sitting in the auditorium. All on his own."

"You know what, Bart? Life's never dull around you."

Ada drags me out into the auditorium. People I don't know come up and say nice things.

"Just enjoy it," Ada whispers in my ear. "Superstar for a day."

Outside in the dark, a shooting star passes, or it might just be a plane or a UFO. It doesn't matter.

I go up the stairs with Grandma, who has been complimenting me all the way home. There's someone sitting outside our door. Grandma grabs my arm.

"Careful," she whispers.

I think I recognize the man in the torn T-shirt with his head on his knees. It is not possible to see whether he's breathing or not. I pull myself loose and go over.

"Geir? Geir?"

His head shoots up and he looks at me with blood-shot eyes.

"You all right?

"Are you all right?" I ask, bending down toward him.

"Well, been better."

"Shouldn't you be in the hospital?

"Not the place for me."

Grandma is standing behind us with a furrowed brow.

"Do you want to come in?"

"Bart," I hear Grandma say, but I ignore her.

"You can't sit out here," I continue.

"No, got my place just down the hall. I'll be fine now. Just wanted to give you this."

He holds a plastic bag out to me. I open it and see there's a black case inside.

"Don't need to open it. It's my old man's watch. A Rolex Oyster Chronographic Antimagnetic from 1952. Engraved on the back."

"But why are you giving it to me?"

"'Cause it's worth a lot of money."

"But . . . don't you need the money?"

"That's the whole point. If I sell it, the money'll go to some damn dealer. I can't . . . bear the thought that that watch just becomes heroin money. You can sell it, and then you and your mom . . . and maybe your grandma too . . . you can move away from here. You shouldn't live here."

"But I can't . . ."

Geir tries to get up.

"Give me a hand. Body's a bit stiff."

I hold Geir under the arm, lose my balance, and just about fall on top of him. Eventually I manage to pull him to his feet. He sways a bit.

"I don't know what to say," I stammer, looking in the bag.

"Don't need to say much. Thanks'll do."

"Thank you."

"My pleasure. Don't turn out like me."

"I promise."

He staggers off down the hall.

"Who is he?" Grandma asks.

I haven't thought about it before now, but there is really only one way to describe Geir. "He's my best friend."

Sometimes you just have to make big decisions in life. I don't know if this is one of them. But I'm going to stop boxing. I haven't got another 9,960 hours of boxing in me.

I must have sung for around 500 hours in the bathroom, and somehow 9,500 hours of singing sounds like much less. There's a small window in the bathroom. I'm going to open it tomorrow when I'm singing.

I sit by Mom's bed at the hospital and look at her sleeping. She makes horsey noises and turns her head a little. When she wakes up, I'm going to tell her about the show. But I'm dreading telling her about the watch. She'll probably say that we have to give it back, and I know that she's right. On the Internet it says that collectors in other countries would pay at least 500,000 kroner for it. What if I were to pay Geir back when I'm grown-up? If he stops taking heroin now, he could probably live until he's eighty.

My cell phone vibrates in my pocket. I leave the room and see that it's Ada.

"This is Bart's live voicemail," I say.

"Hi. What's up?"

"I'm at the hospital. Mom's asleep."

"How's she doing?"

"Better."

"That's good. I was just wondering if you wanted to go to the movies tonight?"

"Maybe."

"I thought I could get one of those two-seater sofas at the Colosseum. The ones at the back. There are still some left for six thirty."

Ada with all the teeth has a boyfriend. He lives somewhere else. He's older. She used to talk about him a lot.

"Yes, we . . . we could do that."

"Good, let's do that, then."

"It'll be . . ."

"Yeah, won't it? I'll order the tickets now. Bye."

I stand there in the middle of the hospital corridor
and realize that I've grown a little. None of my clothes
fit anymore.

It happens.

I just didn't think it would happen to me.

Did you LOVE reading this book?

Visit the Whyville...

Where you can:
- Discover great books!
- Meet new friends!
- Read exclusive sneak peeks and more!

Log on to visit now!
bookhive.whyville.net

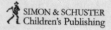

Growing up
with McElderry Books

Solving Zoe
By Barbara Dee

Sand Dollar Summer
By Kimberly K. Jones

Forever Rose
By Hilary McKay

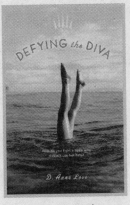

Secret of the Night Ponies
By Joan Hiatt Harlow

The Genie Scheme
By Kimberly K. Jones

Defying the Diva
By D. Anne Love

Margaret K. McElderry Books Published by Simon & Schuster

For Binny it had happened the same way people become friends. Totally. Inevitable from the beginning. Only it was not friends; it was enemies.

★"A well-crafted story that balances moments of hilarity with poignancy."
—*Publishers Weekly*, starred review for *Binny for Short*

★"The writing is gorgeous, clear as water; the characters vivid and lively; the story so real each moment of loss, fear, delight, and love absolutely visceral."
—*Kirkus Reviews*, starred review for *Binny for Short*

★"McKay continues to enthrall readers with her vigorous blend of screwball comedy and heartfelt emotion."
—*Horn Book*, starred review for *Binny in Secret*

★"There's never a dull moment in the Cornwallis household— nor one not rich with love and laughter."
—*Kirkus Reviews*, starred review for *Binny in Secret*